THE FOOL'S JOURNEY

CHRONICLES OF TAROTLAND

KILLIAN WOLF

Grim House
Publishing

ISBN: 978-1-951140-10-6

Copyeditor: Salt & Sage Books - saltandsagebooks.com
Cover design: Logan Keys - coverofdarknessdesign.com
Conlanger: Christian Thalmann
Map designer: Zentra Brice
Header designer: Etheric Designs - etherictales.com/etheric-designs
Formatter: Michael Davie - grimhousepub.com/plans-pricing

For Ash the Silent

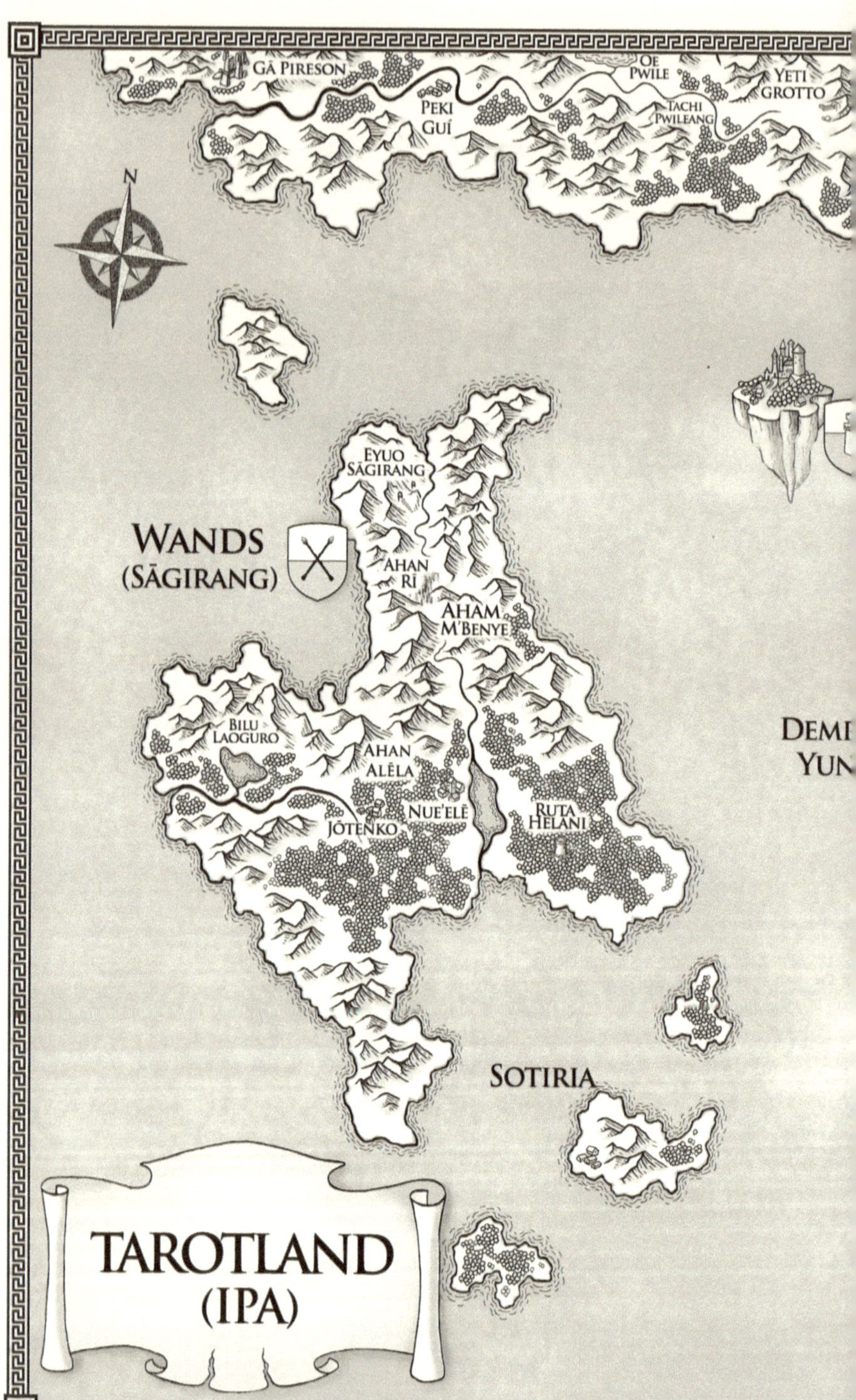

GĀ PIRESON
OE PWILE
YETI GROTTO
PEKI GUÍ
TACHI PWILEANG
N
EYUO SĀGIRANG
WANDS
(SĀGIRANG)
AHAN RĪ
AHAM M'BENYE
BILU LAOGURO
DEME YUN
AHAN ALÊLA
NUE'ELĚ
JŌTENKO
RUTA HELANI
SOTIRIA
TAROTLAND
(IPA)

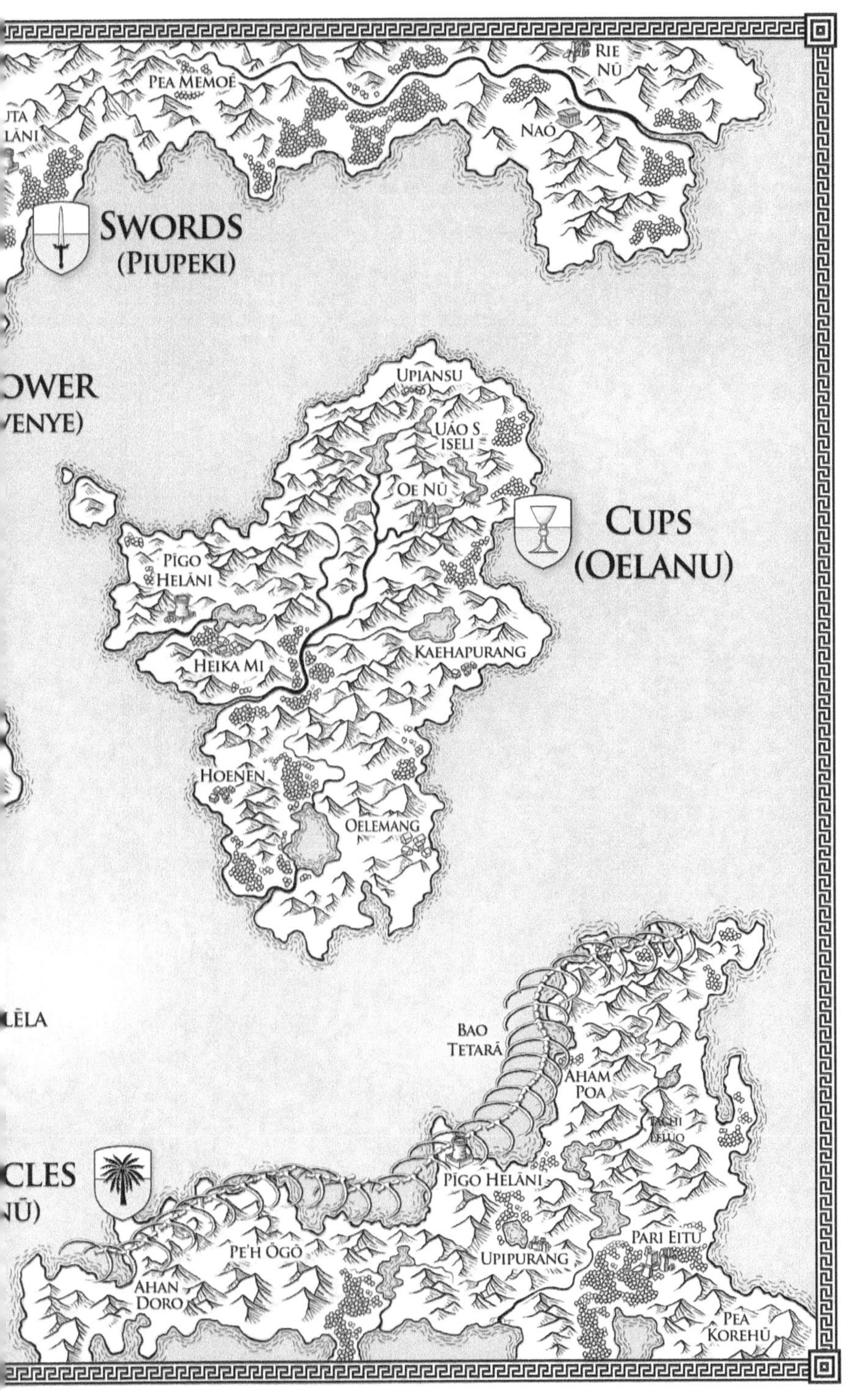

PEA MEMOÉ
RIE NŪ
NAÓ
SWORDS
(PIUPEKI)
OWER
(VENYE)
UPIANSU
UÁO S ISELI
OE NŪ
CUPS
(OELANU)
PĪGO HELÁNI
KAEHAPURANG
HEIKA MI
HOENEN
OELEMANG
LĒLA
BAO TETARÁ
AHAM POA
TACEII DELUO
CLES
(NŪ)
PĪGO HELÁNI
PARI EITU
PE'H ŌGŌ
UPIPURANG
AHAN DORO
PEA KOREHŪ

CHAPTER ONE

THE BURIAL IS THE WORST PART OF THE FUNERAL. I thought it would be standing before my mother's casket, facing family I hadn't seen in years, while she lay still in a box. I thought I would want to run away screaming and never look back. I did, but this is still worse.

The steady beeping of the heart monitor still rings in my ear from the day I stood in that cold hospital room. Even now, in my head I'm standing there, holding my mother's freezing hands, until the very moment the doctor unplugged her from life support.

My aunt Liv was with me in the hospital room; she's been my rock ever since my mom fell into her coma. I don't know if I could ever get through this without her. I remember how she placed a hand on my shoulder and whispered: *"but when the gods tried to speak, they were unable, for they began to weep so that no god could tell another of their agony in words. It's okay to cry, Harold. As did the gods when Baldur died."*

I square my jaw and swallow. Tears sting behind my eyes, but they don't fall. Ever since I could remember, my mother has told me tales of Norse Mythology; it's our heritage, so my guess is she wanted me to know them. The only problem was that she used those tragic and horrible stories as a means to keep me in line. After my aunt moved in, she continued. I really don't want to hear them now.

My hand is starting to sweat from how tightly I hold onto the bundle of daisies. Everyone else is holding roses. But my mom loved daisies.

Mom had been in a coma for so long that seeing her lying still was no different than the past nine years. In fact, at the funeral, I didn't cry at all. I almost felt relieved, but then guilt set in.

But now, seeing this casket about to be lowered six feet under the ground makes it real. At least before, there was hope. Now I wish I could crawl in there with her.

And I don't even know if this makes it worse, but the doctors could never figure out why she went into that coma.

"Would anyone like to say a few words?" The officiant looks over to my father standing next to me.

My father's sunglasses hide his eyes as he clears his throat. "I like to remember her before her illness took her. Thank you all for coming," he makes it short. His voice cracks, and he stares at me. I place a hand on his shoulder. "I will miss her very much."

"We all do, dad. I guess I can say something." Ignoring everyone's stares, I fix my eyes on my mom's rosewood casket. The very expensive rosewood casket is meant to make my mother feel loved and comfortable, even though she's gone forever. It's really to make my father and aunt feel better about having to pull the plug. I don't blame them, though. Her illness reached her brain, and then there was nothing left.

Sweat rolls down my forehead from the hot summer sun. "Thank you all for coming." I clean my throat. "My mother was a strong person. She showed me that even in the darkest times, to use my humor to find the light."

My aunt Liv smiles at me from across the burial, and I keep going.

"The last time I saw my mom smiling was when I was eight years old at the beach. But that's not my favorite memory because that was right before she fell. My favorite memory of her is when she took me to see Batman for the first time. After the movie, we went for milkshakes at Seabreeze Diner, and she told me why Batman was her favorite superhero; it was because no matter how terrible the bad guys were, Bruce would never kill them. He relied on himself to be badass with no superpowers."

"Harold..." My dad mutters.

"Sorry," I say. "If there's anything my mom told me that has stuck with me all these years, it's to always be more like Batman."

My father, however, has never cared for my humor at the worst of times. But I know my mom would have appreciated it.

A few people chuckle, but I don't bother to look up to see who it is. I think I heard my aunt, who's probably wondering if I'm purposely avoiding talking about Norse mythology, despite it having been so important to my mother. She and her sister always had a thing against killing. It always sounded silly to me because who, other than a psychopath, would plan on killing someone? I take the bundle of daisies in my hand and toss them on top of the rosewood casket. "I love you, mommy."

Soft tunes of piano and violin start playing from a speaker. The officiant gives the signal, and the casket starts to get lowered. My chest tightens, and I let myself go numb.

Across from me, my aunt bends down, holding a small black leather pouch in her hands. I squint as she unravels its ties and pulls out a wooden rune. I know it's a rune because I've seen her cast them many times when I was younger, but she hasn't for a long time. Not since she's had to help my dad take care of me; he hates any talk of magic.

The shape of a straight line, the color of ice appears right above her hand. I do a double-take. What the heck? The ice shatters and disappears as it falls to the grass. I blink a few times, and she locks eyes with me.

Did that really happen? Or am I losing it? No one else seemed to notice. I guess I haven't slept much this week, so it's possible I imagined it.

Aunt Liv drops the rune back in her pouch and stands. A bird caws above us, and I glance up to look at my aunt's familiar, Snorri. He circles around and lands on the branch of an oak behind her. She continues to stare at me. I stare back and offer her a smile. It's better than looking down at the casket being buried. A painful look twists her face, and she falls.

"Aunt Liv?" I run to her, passing a few family members who seem just as shocked as I am. A cousin from my dad's side beats me to it and puts his hand under her arm to help her up. I steady her on her other side.

"I'm alright," she says. "Don't worry about me."

"What was that about?" I ask, offering her my arm to keep her steady. She takes it and taps me on my forearm.

"Weak knees." Frost appears on the corners of her eyes, and my brows furrow. I'm definitely not imagining this.

My father walks up behind me. "You alright, Liv?"

"Please, just ignore me. I'm just a little sun fried, is all."

That doesn't explain the frost. Summertime in Massachusetts might require a light jacket, but we'd never see frost under someone's eyes.

My dad switches his gaze to me. "Why don't you take her home, son?"

I nod and give my aunt a pleading look. She sighs in return.

"I was tired anyway," she digs into her purse and hands me her keys. "You drive."

Snorri lands on his perch right outside the kitchen window overlooking the backyard. A crystal suncatcher makes a reflective rainbow dance on the windowsill, catching the crow's attention.

I'm sitting in the kitchen's breakfast nook when Aunt Liv comes out of her room holding a navy-blue leather pouch.

"I want to give you something. Hold out your hand."

I lay my hands on her kitchen table, and she places the leather pouch on my palms.

"This belonged to your mother." She sits on the breakfast bench in front of me, so I'm facing her.

Unraveling its cords, I feel the old leather between my

fingertips. I peer inside and take out a small wooden nub with a rune etched onto it. "My mother read the runes?"

"We both did. Our grandfather taught us both when we were little kids. She would have wanted you to have these." She taps on the rune I pulled out. "That one's called *Uruz*. It means wild ox— like you." She smiles.

I half smile. My mother began calling me a wild ox when I was five because she said I was as rambunctious as one, never listening, always running into trouble. Point me to a five-year-old kid who isn't, though.

"Thank you. I'll take care of them," I say, dropping Uruz back in the bag.

"I know you will. I saw you earlier."

I squint my eyes at her. "What do you mean?"

"You saw me pull out a rune, and you saw what happened, didn't you?"

"I—" The ice had formed a straight line in thin air and then disappeared. "I thought I was seeing things."

"Well, you didn't. You couldn't see it before, back when you used to see me reading them. But now you can."

"What does it mean?"

She gives me a modest shrug. "I suppose it means they're calling to you now that your mother's gone."

I fall silent.

"Usually, a runemaster makes their own. But these share your blood, so you can still bond with them."

"Bond with them?"

"Oh yes, anyone could memorize their names and meanings, but only a true runemaster can bond with each of them, invoke their power, and cast them."

I tie the cord back to how it was and smile at her. I don't know what it means to do any of that.

"Do you remember the bedtime stories I used to tell you?"

"Of Odin, Loki, and Thor? Of course, I remember them all. You *and* my mom shoved them down my throat." Something moves inside the pouch in my hand, and I crinkle my forehead. An image of the Yggdrasil, the world tree, surfaces in my mind. When I was a child Aunt Liv told me tales of the nine realms that circled an impossibly large tree. Why am I thinking of that now?

She frowns, and suddenly I feel bad for upsetting her. "And I appreciate them, Aunt Liv."

"Those are the stories from the Hávamál. If you know the stories, you know the runes." She pauses for a second, looking off to the side. "Do you remember when we went camping, you and I?"

"Of course I do, I was eight years old, and my dad didn't come with us." I know now the reason why he didn't. He needed time to grieve, and Aunt Liv decided it was a good time for us to bond. She's always been fond of the great outdoors.

"And do you remember the fire?"

"I remember you making fire appear without a match and being absolutely amazed at it."

Her lip curls into a smile. "Do you remember what I said before that happened?"

"I remember you muttered a word."

She takes the bag from me and reaches in, rummaging through it. "I called the rune, *Kenaz*. It was your mother's rune." She pulls one out and places it on my palm.

I stare at the wood-burned etching of what looks like the less-than sign in math. "What's it mean?"

"Kenaz is the flame of knowledge—steady and controlled, well-tempered, prepared and ever-burning. She was always studios, your mother. And much more into the runes than I was at a young age." Her brows soften. "You were used to seeing magic once before, Harold. But now, you can see the runes burning when I cast them." She reaches for my arm and lightly brushes it. "You share much more with your mom than just your blonde hair, you know? That burning flame lives within you too. Do you remember what else I told you that day?"

"I think we spoke about a lot of things that day, Aunt Liv."

She rolls her eyes to the sky. "It's what I've always told you to calm you down. To reach into your heart and find its warmth. That's your mother's love. You know it's always there. Sense it. Feel it. I was preparing you to use your magic when the time comes."

"I do remember that." In a way, it was like my mom was there at our camp then. She hands me the pouch, and I place Kenaz inside, tying the leather cord back into a knot.

Frost forms at her lips as she gives three dry coughs. It disappears the moment she stops. She wraps her black cardigan tighter around herself.

"Aunt Liv? What's the matter?"

"I'm okay."

"No, you're not. You collapsed just like mom did during the burial. And—your lips." The memory of my mother collapsing at the beach when I was a kid resurfaces. I push it back and clear my throat. "When did this start?"

She walks over to the kitchen and grabs the kettle. "Tea?"

"Sure. But don't avoid the question."

She fills the kettle with water and places it on the stove. "The night we gave the doctor the okay to do it."

"A week ago? Why didn't you say anything?" I take her arm and lead her to sit on the couch. Aunt Liv is sixteen years older than my mom. She's in fantastic health, eats right, teaches yoga. I shouldn't have to worry about her health. Then again, my mom had been in excellent health too.

"I didn't want to worry you," she says. "With my sister—" Her voice grows heavy, and she shakes her head.

I sit beside her, and for a few minutes, we just stare at the floor in silence.

"I had a terrible feeling this was going to happen to me the night I made the decision about her."

"Aunt Liv, we all agreed it was the right thing to do."

"I know. I'm afraid it's more complicated than that."

"How so?"

The kettle starts to whistle, and my aunt gets up to pour the water into our mugs. Snorri pecks at the glass, and I tap it in response. She sets the mugs on the table but doesn't sit down. The calming fumes of peppermint tea smother my senses. Her eyes stare into the cup as if she's staring into a crystal ball.

"I never thought the curse was real," she says with caution in her tone. "We were always careful just in case. But it seems this curse has always had a way of finding us."

"What are you talking about? What curse?"

"Do you remember how your mom and I repeatedly told you how killing is always wrong?"

I chuckle under my breath. "She did more than that. She made sure I was always the star student, never straying out of line. She'd tell me horror stories of what would happen to children who grew up to be criminals. She showed me photographs of people having been electrocuted or hung. *So did dad.* They even went as far as getting a cop friend of theirs to show me the room they do lethal injections when I was seven." I shiver. "I love my mom, but she had her moments where she went a bit over-the-top morbid, you know? At least you never did any of that."

Her eyes soften.

"It worked, though. I understand the ends never justify the means. Everything leads to death. Theft leads to death. Trespassing leads to death. Even lying leads to death.

"For us, Harold, that may very well be true." She stares at me, a look of determination pasted on her face. "Come with me."

I stand and follow her to her bedroom. The smell of leather-bound books, with a subtlety of old paint, wafts under my nose. Under a window is her art station, with cups of paintbrushes, loose leaf pages, and an easel next to it. She opens a wooden chest inside the closet and starts rummaging through old books. Finally, she takes out a leather-bound journal and hands it to me.

"In these pages, you'll find everything you need to know about the curse. It's up to you if you want to believe it, but I can't shake the feeling there's truth to it."

I open the journal to the front page. Its pages are yellow, and the handwriting is hardly legible. I squint to read the words: *Works of Erling Gundersen, translated by Bjorn Andersen. In dire need of Nauthiz, to quench the curse of murder.*

"Curse of murder?" I glance up from the book.

"I realize now it isn't so literal. The curse takes many forms. In those pages, you'll learn that our ancestors came from another land in the Yggdrassil tree, the World Tree."

"Yes, I know what Yggdrasil means, Aunt Liv. But... this is..." I flip through some more pages. I don't want to tell her how crazy it sounds. Especially not today. Good thing my dad isn't here.

"Just listen," she says. I stop at a page labeled *Breaking the Curse.* "About a year before your mother fell, frost had started forming around her eyes and lips."

I look up from the book. "I'm listening."

"And a year before the day she fell on the beach, a seven-year-old boy had broken into her land with his brother."

"What's that got to do with—"

"The boy's body was found floating in the river. We never told you because it's just such sad news, and we wanted you to focus on school, not add to what you were already dealing with —with your mom in a coma."

"He died? On her property? That's awful."

"Your mother was horrified. She felt so guilty, even though she didn't kill him herself, she always wondered if there should have been better precautions taken to keep people out."

"Aunt Liv, her land is all the way in Wyoming. There's no way she could have done anything."

"And yet she felt negligent. A little boy died, Harold. And your mother always thought, what if it had been you?"

"I understand. But what does this have to do with a curse supposedly placed on our ancestors hundreds of years ago?"

"It was a curse placed on our bloodline by Frost Giants, which said if any one of us takes the life of another, in any form, that person will be dealt with using the same rune. *Isa.* Which means..."

"Ice. I remember. That explains the straight line in the form of an icicle that appeared at the cemetery."

She nods. "That is the rune Isa. I had a gnawing feeling at the back of my mind ever since the day at the hospital when I said goodbye to my sister," her voice grows heavy. "And then the rune showed up."

"But mom had an illness..."

"An illness the doctors couldn't name. They didn't know what was happening to her. They said some people fall into comas." She rolls her eyes. "It just happens, I guess." Her voice raises an octave with last line.

So, safe to say she believes in this curse now. Do I? Can I not? I saw the rune show up when she pulled *Isa* from her bag. I saw the frost form at her eyes and then at her lips. Could it be a coincidence my mother showed symptoms of the curse my aunt describes shortly after the boy died on her land? Or that it's showing now on Aunt Liv after she pulled the plug on my mom? "And what about you? I saw the frost in your eyes. Why is it happening now?"

She blinks and glances down at her feet. "The curse transfers from one to another."

"Say I believe all this," I start. "How would one go about breaking the curse?"

"Oh Harold, I am only telling you all this so you can stay

vigilant about not accidentally killing someone." She sighs. "You would have to take someone's life. I would never want that for you. Your mother would never want that for you. Your whole life, we've been trying to shield you from accidentally enacting it. Don't do it on purpose and throw away your life."

My eyes widen. "So that's it, huh? Kill someone and transfer your curse to me. There's no other way?"

"Unfortunately, your great grandfather," she points to the book, "never found a way to break it. It says in there that the Frost Giants cast our ancestors out of Jotunheim for good. To break it—and not just transfer it, would mean to travel to Jotunheim and face the Frost Giants who cast it. The only way there would be for a runemaster who has never committed murder to open a portal."

"Well, lucky for us, I have never killed anyone—wait, do animals count?" They can't count. None of us are vegetarians.

She shakes her head. "Eating a roast won't enact the curse, but Harold, you would have to be a runemaster to open such a portal."

"Is that part really important?"

"How would you go in without having bonded with the runes? You'd have to open a portal to *another world*. And it wouldn't be easy. There are countless other worlds." She places her hands on her hips and smiles. "Not to mention, if such a thing were possible, it would be dangerous. I wish I had taught you more directly, but your father never allowed it."

"Hey, I've been taking martial arts since I was ten. I'm sure I can face off a few Frost Giants." I wink. She shakes her head.

I close the journal and hand it back to her. "If such a thing were possible, Aunt Liv, I wouldn't think twice about going if it would give me a chance to save you from the curse."

"And anyone else in our family who becomes as unfortunate. If nothing else, maybe that little boy would have lived."

"What are you saying? That maybe it was because of the curse the kid was attracted to my mom's land?"

She shrugs. "Our cosmic energy affects others, you know. Keep the journal; learn as much as you can. It's the only thing that can keep you and your future children safe. It's too late for me now."

Later, I keep my dad company until he falls asleep. But after he gets up to go to bed, I lie in my room with the journal open.

I don't know if I believe in curses, but I admit what my aunt was saying helps fit some of the icy pieces together. I flip to the back of the journal to the page that has all the runes listed, with their meanings of how to read them and what they could do if cast. The first one is *Fehu: A monetary exchange; cattle. Can be used to supercharge Uruz in order to heal.* My eyes grow heavy, and I fall asleep.

I jerk awake. "What?" I thought I heard something. It sounded like something rumbling. I yawn and rub my eyes. A bright light is coming from my desk. I stare at it, still not fully awake. Leaning a bit closer, the blue leather pouch of runes rumbles. I squint at it, and it rumbles again.

Now I'm awake.

I bolt out of bed and make it across my room, nearly tripping over my sheets. Light seeps out from the opening, so I unravel the cord, remembering the rune from Aunt Liv's bag earlier in the cemetery. One by one, fiery lights in the shape of the runes start flying out of the bag.

I duck as they zip over my head.

Not the physical wooden nubs that are still in the bag; this is as if their spirit forms are rising as fiery glyphs. I pinch myself to make sure I'm not dreaming.

The runes form a large circle in front of my wall. I take a few steps backward toward my bedroom door.

The center of the circle flickers in and out until it becomes a solid, black void.

What the actual hell is going on?

A spot of color appears in its center. I rub my eyes again, disbelief still in the forefront of my mind. I pinch myself again, but you know how in dreams sometimes you think you feel pain? I can't be too sure. My eyes widen as that spot of color gets bigger until I can make out a bark and leaves. The tree grows as it spins. As it gets closer, land masses come into view, showing nine realms held in large branches along the length of the tree. A large rainbow emerges from behind the tree and wraps around, ending right at the opening of the circle.

A cold wind smacks my face as I stare at the glistening colors of the rainbow bridge.

Aha. Yeah, no. A big fat nope! I have completely lost it. I smack myself hard.

Lightning strikes inside the portal, sending an earth-shattering roar. I nearly jump out of my skin and bolt out of my room, slamming the door behind me. Leaning with my back against my bedroom door, my heart hammers in my chest.

This can't be happening. That didn't just happen. I mean,

none of this can be real. I wanted to believe Aunt Liv about the curse, but... this is impossible, right? Isn't it?

On the count of three, I'm going to open the door again, and all of it will be gone. It's my imagination. One. Two. I spin around, twist the doorknob, and open the door. Three.

The rainbow bridge is still there, inside the circle of fiery runes. The bark of the tree is now so enlarged that I can't see the rest of it. I shut the door again. "Aunt Liv!" My voice cracks as I sprint down the hall, through the living room, and swing her door open. She's sound asleep. I Approach her bed and turn on her bedside lamp. "Aunt Liv?"

Frost covers the corner of her eyelids. I hold her hand; it's icy to the touch. She stirs awake.

"Harold?"

Her blue eyes have a tint of gray in them that wasn't there before, almost as if ice is making its way inside her eyes. I shudder a breath... "this curse is real, isn't it?"

She squints from the brightness of the lamp. "What's the matter? Are you alright?"

"It's all real, isn't it? Tell me."

She blinks a few times and rubs the frost from her eyes. "I believe it is."

Should I tell her about the open portal in my room? Am I actually considering going in? I take a deep breath. "If there was a way to cross worlds, how would I break the curse?"

"Well, I don't know," she says. "I suppose trust in the runes for the right path. I would let them lead me to where the curse first began," her voice becomes firmer, emanating the story-teller and runemaster I remember from my childhood. "I would confront the curse maker and find a way to break it.

Why do you ask?" She looks at the clock on her bedside table. "At one in the morning."

"Do you know why our ancestors killed one of theirs?" I need more answers if I'm going to aimlessly cross to another world.

She shakes her head, concern reaching her eyes. "I'm sorry, but I don't. It happened too long ago, and I never thought any of it was real. Why the sudden interest?"

Can I do this? Find the Frost Giants who cursed my family and ask them to lift it? Possibly fight them to the death? Will they still be around? I mean, they're Frost Giants. They're probably immortal.

"I'm sorry, Liv, I couldn't sleep," I lie. I lean in and give her a hug. "I love you."

"I love you too, Harold."

I'll leave her a note. I'm not going to risk her trying to talk me out of it because it's too dangerous, or worse, her trying to come with me.

I have to go in. It's the right thing to do, and this might be the only way to avenge my mother's death and make sure my aunt doesn't fall into the same fate.

CHAPTER TWO

 Strong winds push at my hair from around the bark of the world tree, only now it seems to be getting smaller. I think it's closing.

Dashing into the depths of my closet, I pull out my backpack and grab a winter coat because mythical Norwegian lands equal snow. I pack a few essentials, my pocketknife, and the journal my aunt gave me. It's the only manual I have to navigate these foreign lands and learn the runes.

The lights from the rune circle start to flicker, and my pulse quickens. Reaching over a pile of history and archaeology books, I grab a pen and a notepad.

Dear Aunt Liv,
It looks like the stories are true, and the runes opened a
portal. I'll be over the rainbow bridge trying to

right our ancestor's wrongs. Please take care of
my dad.
Love,
Harold

What are the chances she'll be okay with this? The portal
lights flicker again, and I swing my backpack on. I hold my
mother's rune pouch in my hands. I'm really doing this. I look
behind me. My bedroom door is still closed, and the lights on
the other side are still off.

Everything leads to death.

Here's to hoping this doesn't. I take one deep breath and
cross the threshold.

As I step through, my feet land on an invisible barrier
beneath me. Bright blues, greens, yellows, oranges of the
rainbow bridge wrap around in a beautiful spiral, disappearing
all the way up the tree's bark, following massive branches to
different lands.

I take my next step, and I'm completely inside the portal now,
gripping the bark of Yggdrasil. From memory, I know Jotunheim
is all the way to the bottom left. I start sliding my way toward the
left, to Jotunheim. I crane my neck to look back at the portal
closing when electricity zaps at my hands, and I let go of the bark.

I gasp as a force field flings me backward. Panic surges up
my spine as the last thing I see is my aunt—horror stricken,
right as the portal closes.

"Aunt Liv!"

My arms fling upward, and my backpack swings over my
head. And I gain speed.

I try to grab onto something. Anything. My fingers burn as friction abrades my skin, forcing me to let go.

I fall quickly down an endless black void. The image of Yggdrasil growing farther away.

Quicker by the moment, I fall until my blood rushes to my head, and I land on what feels like a rope.

My hands grab onto something sticky that bounces me up and down. I lift my fingers and pull on a white, translucent thread. Not rope. What the hell is this? I try spinning myself around to try and stand, but the more I do, the more the string-like material sticks to me. I search the dark void around me. The only thing lit is the illuminating netting I'm sitting on, each string loops around the other, creating an endless net, like one big... web.

Please don't tell me I'm on a spider web.

The web moves around me, and I curse under my breath. This is not what I signed up for. I take a deep breath and glance behind me.

That's when I see my reflection in way too many eyes staring back at me from a spider triple the size of me with a big, bulbous body. As it moves, more of my reflection comes into view, and for a second, I think there's more of them. But then I notice its body has a unique mosaic pattern of black glass shards.

Panic soars through my veins as I take in all of it. The tiny hairs on its legs. The idea it could pounce on me at any moment. The way its fangs move under its hairy face. My hands start to shake, and slowly, I feel for my pocketknife in my belt loop.

I start slicing at the thread, trying not to make sudden

movements. I cut at the sticky netting under my left arm, and the spider twitches its legs, watching my every move with its many eyes.

I'm going to try to get as loose as I can to somehow climb up the web and find the tree.

I have no idea if that's even possible, but at this point, I have no idea what to do.

I reach for my legs, and the spider flinches, causing me to nearly jump out of my skin. The web shakes and startles the spider.

Its eight legs start to move at a terrifying speed, and I choke on a scream.

I fight to move back, and as I do, the web beneath me gives way. Once again, I begin to fall.

My eyes fling open as I spit snow out of my mouth in ice-chattering coughs.

A cold weight presses down on my back, and it takes me a moment to realize that it's just my heavy coat, now wet and covered in snow. And not a giant spider.

Relieved, I push myself up with my arms. Holy hell, I have snow everywhere, and I do mean *everywhere*.

Reaching into my shirt inside my coat, I shake off the snow from my undergarments and legs. Gods, that's freezing.

I look up to the sky and squint at the sun. Where the hell did I fall from? The last thing I remember was falling through the spider web and then... Landing was a blur.

I spot my backpack on a snow-covered bush and pick it up.

I guess I made it after all. A winter hell where I managed to get snow on my balls? Seems legit.

A sinking feeling weighs down on my stomach.

Aunt Liv was flung back when she tried to reach me. She sure picked a time to go check on me. For a split second, I'm thankful she has the curse on her. Otherwise, she'd be able to open the portal and come after me. She's better off safe from danger and home. Also, she'll keep my dad from filing a missing person's report.

Swinging my backpack over my shoulder, I take a good look at my surroundings to try and orient myself. A large, broken column leaning on the ground catches my eye. My gaze follows it to a platform, and I trudge toward it. Looks like some kind of ruin.

More broken-down columns between trees and broken pieces of the stone ground make way as I get closer. Three tall columns stand unbroken as I climb onto the center of the ruins. My eyes follow the columns to the top and stop at an oddly familiar decorum. The famous ionic rolled marble, under a flat surface. I remember reading about them when I was interested in Greek archaeology. But this doesn't make any sense. Why would there be Greek ruins in Jotunheim?

Something crunches underfoot. My eyes skim the ground and pass an engraved tile with the image of a curved web.

Unless I never made it into Jotunheim.

I rub my chin. I couldn't have made it; I never went left to get to Jotunheim. A force field sent me crashing down into a giant web. I open my eyes again and stare at the spiderweb insignia. Panic competes with the cold sinking in my blood.

What's the probability that I ended up in a completely

different world, other than any world held by Yggdrasil? Are there even more worlds? I mean, if Yggdrasil is real, why wouldn't there be more? How do I even figure out where I am?

I spin around, looking up at the sky as if I could somehow find a way to climb back up. Taking out the rune pouch, I hold it in front of me.

"Go on, you opened a portal before. Do it again." Nothing happens. I unravel the drawstring and open it up. "Come on, we have to get out of here. If not Yggdrasil, then at least take me home."

A cold breeze passes through my hair, and the only noise I hear is the crunch of my shoe against the snow. I peer inside the bag. Before in my room, they rumbled, and their spirits started flying around the room. Now, they don't even look mystical. Like they're just wooden nubs with carvings on them. "Did you break?" I yell, and the sound of my voice echoes through the mountains.

Okay, get a hold of yourself, Harold. There has to be a way out of this mess. I have a bag full of magical runes. I just need to figure out how to use them.

A low-pitched bell-like tune rings in my ear.

Ah, now I have tinnitus. Makes sense since I just fell who knows how many stories and am somehow still alive.

The ringing intensifies as I walk, so I press my hand tightly against my right ear. Wait a minute. That's not coming from my ear.

I spin around, and the ringing grows louder. Peering through the ruined structure, I stare into the vast mountain ranges covered in snow and alpines. I can't tell where they're coming from. My options are to walk in a random direction and hope to make it to a village or stay put and freeze. I have no idea which way to start walking. I could be walking for days.

What would my aunt want me to do?

Trust in the runes for the right path. The ringing gets louder as I undo the leather drawstring. It's coming from the runes. I walk back to the stone platform and wipe the surface with my hand before taking a seat.

Though I've seen my aunt read them as a form of divination and cast them countless times, I'm at a loss of where to begin. Turning to my backpack, I start digging for the journal. When I find it, I flip through the pages until I find one that reads:

Guidance for Divination

What comes after that is familiar to me. I swear I've heard my aunt say these words before. This feels right.

A cold breeze passes through my hair, running shivers down my arms and legs. I read the passage a few times until I can recall it in my mind. Then, holding the pouch of runes in my left hand, I close my eyes and concentrate.

"I call upon Skuld, who holds our future in her hands,

I call upon Verdandi, who wraps our present in her warm embrace,

I call upon Ord, who shrouds our past in the deep folds of her cloak.

Odin, lend me your eye so that I may read the runes aright."

I open my eyes, and the ringing has stopped.

Alright, my question is... Where do I go from here in order to get to Jotunheim?

With my right hand, I start pulling out three runes, one at a time, as per instructions in the journal.

Hagalaz, Nauthiz, Jera.

I flip the pages to the back of the journal with their definitions. My mind blanks. Seriously? Tell me something I don't know. Hagalaz: a drastic change just happened. Check. Nauthiz: dire need of a fire, yeah no shit, check. And Jera, having to work at what I need. Good for nothing runes. I put back Hagalaz and Nauthiz, keeping Jera in my hand. "How 'bout some advice this time?"

This time I pull out one rune: *Uruz.*

My brows furrow. Uruz? That's the rune my aunt said represents me. But what it actually means is wild ox. "Are you runes telling me I'm on my own?"

I shove the rune back in the pouch and stand up. Looks like I'm on my own then. Seek their guidance. How am I meant to do that if they're telling me what I already know?

Bond with them.

I shake my aunt's voice out of my head. I don't know how to bond with twenty-four wooden nubs. What am I meant to do? Take them all out on a date? Things couldn't get any worse.

I turn around and find a sharp spear pointed right at my chest.

My eyes follow the pointed blade to the girl who's holding it. She has fierce dark eyes and matching long wavy hair with cheekbones for days. I lock eyes with her; she's strikingly beautiful.

Subtly pointed ears stick out between strands of her hair. That's different.

"*Twae po?*" she says. Accusation is in her tone, even though I have no idea what she just said. My eyes move to the sharp double fangs inside her mouth.

Woah.

I lift my hands in a surrender stance. She adjusts a rope tied over her left shoulder filled with what looks like dead rabbits.

She repeats what she said.

"I'm sorry, I don't understand," I say. "Can you please lower your weapon?"

Her brows scrunch, and she nudges the point at me harder.

"Woah," I step back.

"*Temū,*" she barks.

She nudges me, and I take it as a cue to walk.

"Look, I don't mean you harm. Even though you're the one attacking me right now. I need some help."

She pokes me with the point.

"Ow! Hey, stop that." I block the spear with my right hand, snapping it away from me. This startles her, and she sweeps me off my balance with her foot. I land on my ass.

She starts yelling wildly at me, and I lift myself up, my hands up in front of me.

"I'm sorry," I say.

"*Oete.*" She nudges me with her spear again, and I start to walk. She occasionally shouts something and urges me forward with the point of her spear.

"You really don't need to do that. I have nowhere to go anyway." And hopefully, she's leading me to a village where I can ask for help. However, there being a language barrier hadn't occurred to me.

She leads me down a thickly wooded forest until we get to

an incline, and I follow her up an incredibly steep hill. Had I not been fit, I would have found this challenging. But I work out a lot, so it's cool.

Not really. I'm dying. And I need water. I reach into my backpack for my water bottle, and as expected, she barks something at me.

"It's just water. See?" I show her my water bottle and take a drink. She purses her lips and keeps walking.

We reach the top of the mountain to a small tree house overlooking the vast land of this world. Mountain ranges wall in what looks like a large canal leading to the ocean far away. A bit closer, though, is a village, starting to light up in the setting sun.

Something wraps around my neck and pulls me back. I grab at my neck and pull on a smooth plant-like rope. "What—hey! What are you doing?"

She grabs me from behind, and I fly back into a hard surface. It takes me a moment to realize she's tied me to a tree at warp speed.

Whoever this girl is, she's a wicked good huntress.

"I told you I wasn't going anywhere." Not that she could understand me. She makes her way around me, tying the forest green plant rope tighter around my waist. "I haven't even taken you to dinner yet."

She furrows her brows and stares up at me. I chuckle, not being able to hide the smirk on my face. Maybe she understood my intonation?

She stands and points the spear at my throat. "Koj oete."

"Yeah, don't move? Something or other. Got it." Now, if I

can only reach my pocketknife and cut myself loose, I'll be making my exit.

She reaches down and starts patting the sides of my pants, finding my pocketknife securely tucked inside my belt.

"Oh, come on!"

She then squeezes the outside of my pocket and reaches in to pull out my pouch of runes. My heart plummets to my stomach. Oh no. She opens the leather bag and furrows her brows, stopping to glance up at me.

"I need those."

She doesn't seem to care to try and understand me, and I'm sure if I add a pretty please to that statement, it won't matter.

With her spare hand, she tugs on the rope, and after seeming pleased with her handy work, she turns to leave inside her winter tree house.

Snow starts to fall, and a cold wind smacks my face.

"Wait. You're not going to leave me here all night, are you?"

She disappears up her tree and in through a door. "You're kidding me, right?" Seriously? What harm was I doing to her just being out there? "Hey!" I yell. "You can't leave me out here to freeze!"

A wolf howls from the direction of the woods behind me. I'm not about to become wolf chow. I start twisting frantically, trying to get loose. But the harder I try to get free, the tighter the rope becomes.

CHAPTER THREE

Icicles are forming at the edge of my eyes like the Misty Mountain peak, Caradhras in Lord of the Rings. Not only that, but I've also managed to twist all the air out of my gut, and it's getting harder to breathe. What kind of magic is this? Not that I'm familiar with anything but the runes—well, okay, hardly even that, but… this is like Poison Ivy let one of her live vines loose on me.

Have I mentioned I cannot feel my fingers or toes?

On the horizon, the sun is dipping behind the mountain tops. How long have I been out here?

A door opens, and I move my neck to see, causing the rope vine to tighten around me more. The native girl who tied me up climbs down her tree house with one arm, a cup in the other.

"Aw, how sweet. I hope that's a hot drink."

She makes her way over to me, wrinkles in her forehead permanently pasted from her furrowed brows.

"Hey, while you're at it, would you mind loosening up your handy work? I kind of need to breathe."

She stares at me inquisitively. The fur from her coat covers half her face as the wind blows in from the cliffside. My pouch of runes is tied to her wrist as she holds it up and says something to me I can't understand. I shake my head.

The girl steps closer and holds the cup up to my face. "Indakepoa garisi."

My throat is parched, so I let her hold the cup to my lips. At this point, why poison me? She already has me tied up. I could literally freeze to death. The lukewarm drink touches my tongue, and I immediately start to gag from the unexpectant taste of licorice.

"Awe, why would you do that?" I spit. Drool hangs from my lips. Charming. I don't actually mind licorice; it's just not what I wanted when I was expecting water.

"Drink all of it," she says.

I gasp. "Have you been able to speak English this whole time?"

She shakes her head. "Drink."

I screw up my face.

"It is a language potion. Now," she nudges the cup back to my face, "drink."

A language potion? Well, that's awesome. I take a deep breath and guzzle down the rest. My throat burns from the warm licorice sizzling down my dry throat.

"You wouldn't happen to have water, would you?"

Ignoring my question, she unravels my rune pouch from her wrist and opens them. "What are these?"

"Those are mine. And I'm going to need you to give them back."

She moves forward and tugs on the rope, causing it to restrict tighter. "Are they ouma?"

I cough from the rope constricting me like a snake. "I don't know what that means."

"Magic."

"Yes, they are magic. How come I couldn't understand you just then?"

"The potion works on one language only. Lucky for you, I speak both. Where did you come from?"

A magic potion that only works on one language? That is something I'll have to come back to. "I take it you get lots of foreigners if you have a potion that translates."

"I have never met anyone not from Ipa. You are the first. But... there are stories of others. What is your mark?"

"My what?"

She reaches for my wrist and tries to move my sleeve up but can't due to the rope. The harder she pulls, the tighter it gets.

"I don't know what that is, and you're killing my circulation," I tell her as she lets go and scrunches her features.

My teeth chatter. As much as I want to marvel at the coolness of all this magic, I'm freezing my balls off. "This all sounds super interesting. Do you mind if we take it inside? Where it's warm?" Please, please, please say yes.

She takes a step back, uncertainty pasted on her face.

"I'm not here to hurt anyone. I have to find..." My teeth chatter some more. "My way back."

"Where are you trying to go?"

That's a good question. At this point, am I trying to get back home? No. I haven't given up. I need to get the portal to open and go to Jotunheim, but I don't know why I couldn't reach it in the first place. I was so close. Could this girl help me? It's a long shot, but... "I'm on a mission to break my family's curse. I was going to a place called Jotunheim. Have you heard of it?"

She squints her eyes at me as if considering whether or not I'm telling the truth. "I have not heard of this Jotun...eim."

"Look, you can keep me tied up inside if you want."

"Tell me how you came here first."

"That's kind of a long story..."

She lifts her chin and looks back at her house.

"I was trying to go to a different world, but something blocked my entrance, and I fell into a web... then somehow landed here. But I don't know how."

"A web?"

"Yeah, with a very big spider."

"Muse."

"Yeah, *musey*. Whatever that means."

"Muse means spider." She sighs hesitantly and lifts her brows, arching her gaze back to her house.

Just as I think she's going to go back in, she takes out a large knife and sticks it underneath the rope tied around my waist. Before she cuts it, she bores her eyes into mine, twisting the blade against the skin of my stomach. "Any funny business, and I will kill you."

I swallow. "Got it."

She slices the vine. My arms and legs loosen up, and I fall to the ground, barely able to hold myself up. I think I might have frostbite.

"Thank you," I whisper between chattering teeth. Beneath me, the vine convulses and shrivels up. I steady myself up, daring to trust my knees. "Is it...dying?"

"Yes, I enchanted it with ouma, but that potion can only last so long." My eyes widen. She enchanted it with a magic potion. I blink slowly. So, magic is common in this world, and you can enchant things... Like translation potions. Maybe I'm not completely out of luck. What's the possibility of a different way to open a portal here? She seems to know her way around magic. Maybe she can help me.

She starts walking to her tree house, and I try to keep up. She climbs her ladder, and I do the same, with one wet, icy glove after the other. I'm not sure how I feel about winter tree houses, but so far, this feels dangerous.

Inside, the warmth of a cast-iron burner oven heats up the entire two-story treehouse. The aroma of cooked meat greets me as my eyes land on wide wooden shelves holding bottles and bottles of different colored solutions. A table next to the entryway we just walked in has a journal, map, empty bottles, a burner, and a pot filled with clear liquid. Notes of licorice come from that direction, blending in with the aroma of her dinner. A spiral staircase wraps over a wooden beam at the far left corner of the room, leading to a second floor.

"Nice place."

She hasn't moved from the door, staring at me with fierce intensity. Something rattles next to the stove area, and I look past her at a closed brown curtain. "What's through there?"

"You will not go in there. Ever."

"Sounds like some kind of animal in a cage or something. Do you have a pet?"

"Stay away from there." She snaps.

I hold my hands up. "Just making conversation."

She takes my mother's runes in her hands and nudges them at me. "Explain this."

"Those are my runes."

"Your magic?"

"Yeah, yes. Exactly. And they were my mother's, so be careful with them. If I can somehow get them to reopen the portal that got me here, I'll be gone from this world."

"Open a portal," she says slowly. "To Jotun…"

"Jotunheim."

"With these?" She jiggles the contents of the bag.

I nod. "Yes, but they didn't work earlier when I tried. Something happened, and I think I'm stuck here unless I can figure out how to get them to work again."

"So that you can break your family's curse."

"Are you familiar with curses?"

"That would depend on the curse."

"My aunt is very sick," I start. I tell her about my mother having passed away and the curse bestowed on us by the Frost Giants. "Getting to Jotunheim seems to be my only chance at freeing my family and myself from this fate. Unless you know a way to break curses? Have any magical fix-all potions?" I skim the contents of her potion table.

"I'm afraid it won't work that way. It sounds like the quest you are on is the one you need to continue. Portals in this world are not common. They are guarded."

"By spiders?"

"By the Empress. The spiders are hers. I only know of this from tales told to us from birth. I know nothing about opening portals besides knowing that they are illegal. What is your mark?"

"Illegal?" I rub my hands together for warmth. She reaches for a blanket thrown on a few cushions on the floor and hands it to me.

"You should take off your wet clothes."

Already unzipping my jacket, I wrap the blanket over me.

"Show me your mark."

"You keep saying that, but I have no idea what that means."

She flips her wrist over and shows me a dark tattoo of five swords spanning out like a fan.

"Oh...neat. Yeah, I don't have that." I hold my wrist up and show her. "See?"

She raises her brows and steps back. "È? You're a Magician?"

"What?" I flick my eyes to my wrist and deadpan. A Roman number "I" in a tan color has suddenly appeared on my skin. What the heck? "Okay, I'm totally confused.

"Everyone has a mark. Yours is illegal."

I scratch my head as I inspect this strange marking on my wrist, switching from mine to hers. "Wait, what do you mean illegal?"

"Magic is outlawed. And you're a magician." She starts walking toward her door. "You should go."

"Wait, wait, wait. What do you mean magic is outlawed? What about all the potions here and the one you gave me to drink? And I'm," I chuckle nervously, "I'm no magician." Not a very good one, at least. "Did I just drink some illegal potion?" *Everything leads to death.* Everything and anything illegal. First time going through a portal, and I've already slipped up. I'm going to enact the curse and die before I ever make it to Jotunheim.

"Magic here has been outlawed since long before my grandparents were born. Ever since the Helāni conquest. Any magician will be executed by the Empress."

"Hold up. What kind of conquest? Empress? Executed?"

"Helāni is the Ipani word for Greek."

Okay, now the Greek columns are making sense. "So, this isn't some type of Ancient Greek world?"

"It is and has always been Ipa first." She hisses.

"Woah, calm down. I don't know any of this."

She shifts her weight.

I'm in an alternate universe where the Greeks invaded another dimension. Holy shit balls. That is... Really. Freaking. Cool. My nerd senses are begging to come out, but I push them back down. "So, when did the Greeks invade?"

"A very long time ago. It has been this way since before my great grandparents were born." She crosses her arms. "How is it in your world?"

I chuckle. "Well, for starters, we don't have magic like this in my world." I point to my bag. "Those are rare. I'd really like those back, and would prefer not to fight you for them."

She huffs. "It wouldn't be much of a fight. You were easy to tie." She hands me back my mother's runes and I snatch them from her hand, quickly tucking them back in my pocket.

Odin's balls. Her tongue is almost as dangerous as her spear. I love it. "Yeah well, for your information, I can fight. You caught me by surprise, is all."

"Uh huh." She arches a brow and folds her arms in front of her. I skim the bottles.

"The potion you gave me, isn't that magic?"

"Yes."

"And the magical rope-vine thingy?"

"Also ouma."

"Ouma is magic?"

"Yes."

"So how come you don't have the magician's mark?"

"Because I was bound. A magician's magic comes from within. It isn't enough to mix potions."

Magic comes from within. "What does that mean—that you were bound?"

She looks to the side and sighs loudly as she takes off her winter coat and hangs it on a branch sticking out from the wall. "I am half-Ipani, and half human. My biological father was Ipani, but my biological mother was human and spoke Imboe." She moves her hair from her neck, revealing some more birthmarks. These are long, wavy stripes forming at her neck and reaching down to her clavicle. A few more reach down to her hands from underneath her long tunic. "My ama is also human, which is why I speak both Ipani and Imboe. She's my second mother."

Half human and half...Ipani. Pointy ears, sharp teeth, stripes on skin. Got it. "What is Imboe?"

"It is a mixture of Ancient Greek and Ipani. No one speaks Ancient Greek anymore. Except probably the Empress."

The Empress...I shift in place.

"You can sit," she says over her shoulder.

"Thanks, I'm Harold."

"I'm Kenjō."

"Nice to meet you...Now that I'm not tied up, that is." I

chuckle, but she stays quiet. "So, why did you feel like capturing and tying me up? Why not just let me be?"

Her face hardens. "I thought maybe you were the one killing the villagers."

My brows raise. "Definitely not." Does that mean there's a serial killer on the loose? I inch toward the furnace and spread my hands in front of it. I close my eyes to the heat defrosting my face. This feels good. Where do I know these Roman numerals from? The Magician.... the Empress... the Five of Sword! No way. Those are from the Tarot cards. But how is this even possible?

"This curse of yours..."

I snap my attention back to her.

"It is a noble thing you are doing. To make things right with those your blood history wronged."

"I suppose? I'm just trying to—"

"There is a sword that might be able to open a portal."

"A sword that can open a portal?"

"They say it requires a sacrifice for its magic to work. They say the sword has the magic to do anything, so why not open a portal? But you cannot get caught going there. That sword is highly guarded, è?"

I blink. A sword that requires a sacrifice. This sounds right up my alley; the Northmen were all about sacrifices. I'm sure the runes would approve. "Where's this sword?"

"In *Naó*, the Greek Temple. A week's journey East of Pea Memoé, the Eternal Mountains."

A week's journey through *eternal mountains?*

"Usually, I would have you go hunt your own rabbit. But

seeing as how I doubt you can hunt, and you have no knowledge of where you are…"

My eyes widen. "Hey, I can hunt… probably."

"And you seem to bring me no harm."

"I promise you I don't."

She squints her eyes at me. "I will feed you."

"Yay. Can I make it up to you? Tomorrow?"

"Tomorrow, you will leave. Too many killings happen around here at night, so we cannot go anywhere. It is safer inside."

"Right… the killings."

She hands me a small bowl with chunks of meat inside broth. I take it from her, and she sits down next to me.

"Thanks," I say. "I've never eaten rabbit before. It smells good."

She nods and stabs the meat with her knife, bringing it up to her mouth. I take the knife she left in my bowl. I guess they don't have forks in this world. Or maybe only she doesn't. We eat in silence as the events of the day reflect in my mind. Tomorrow I'm off to the Eternal Mountains to find a heavily guarded sword that could open my portal. I could be searching for weeks or months, not knowing how to get there. I turn the meat over as I stare at it.

"Are you not hungry?"

I glance at her to see her licking over her fangs with her tongue. "Yeah, sorry." I take a bite of the rabbit. "I was just thinking… since you know the area, maybe you can come with me?"

"To the Ace of Swords?"

Ace of Swords. It's another card from the Tarot. That's interesting. "I'll find some way to repay you."

She shakes her head. "I do not go through Pea Memoé."

"Why not?"

"Too dangerous."

That doesn't leave me with much confidence. If this girl was able to tie me up and almost kill me, I'll never make it out of this world alive. *And* there's a killer on the loose. I place the bowl down on the floor and take out my mother's runes, hoping that by opening them, they'd all come out like before and open a portal. When nothing happens, I close my eyes and put my hand inside the pouch. I don't even know what to ask. How about, will I make it out of here alive? No, that's a future question. My aunt would snap at me for that. *I make my fate, request advice only,* she'd say.

Okay, I got it. Should Kenjō come with me to find the Ace of Swords?

I pull out a wooden rune and turn it over. *Isa.* I drop it back in the pouch, frowning. What do they know? Isa usually comes out as a one rune pull to mean a simple no. It also means yield or ice. Unless it's referring to the curse of Isa. The memory of the icicle forming in thin air during the burial comes to mind.

"What are you doing?"

I glance up to find Kenjō staring at me intently.

"Oh, I was just asking my ru-uh-magic if you should come with me tomorrow."

She shakes her head.

"They say you should," I smile despite my lie. I shouldn't joke. Even lying leads to death for my family.

"I will not go. I am sorry."

"That's okay. I don't want to put you in danger. Would you be able to give me a map of where I could find the Ace of Swords?" I tuck my mother's runes away in my pocket. Looks like they'll be getting what they want. Me on my own.

She pushes herself up from her seat and leans over to grab my bowl from the floor. I get up to help, taking the bowl back and walking over to the si— uh... "Where do you wash your dishes?"

She points to two metal buckets on the floor, both filled with water, one soapy, one not.

I reach for her bowl and take it from her. "Let me help." She lets go of her bowl with a surprised look on her face. "I like to help," I smile. "And you're being really nice to me."

She blushes, and her gaze moves away from me. "I am going to the village tomorrow," she says suddenly. "I can take you that far and point you in the direction of the forest you need to go to. But then you are on your own."

"I'll take it. Thank you!" After a few moments of her standing there watching me, I start making conversation again. Mostly because I feel awkward with her staring at me and also because she looks conflicted about her taking me. "You're sure this isn't a problem?"

"No, it is fine. I am running low on an ingredient I need, and tomorrow my forager is to meet me there anyway."

"Oh, for your potions?"

She nods.

"More language translator?"

She shakes her head. "You were lucky I had the ingredients for that. And the recipe. I never have to make it."

I dip the bowls in the soapy bucket and wash them with a cloth hanging from its ridge, then rinse them off in the clean water bucket. I hand her the clean bowls, and she takes them from me.

"There's a lot of bottles here. What kind of stuff do you make?"

She twists her lips.

"A secret too, huh?" I'm guessing it has something to do with what's behind that curtain. "Remember, I literally don't know anything about your world. I don't have anyone I could tell, even if I would. But I wouldn't. You can trust me."

She bites her upper lip and then says, "the plant is called Rikorō. Its literal translation in Ipani means soul-eater. Let's just say it is also for healing, but not of the physical body."

"Interesting. I'd love to learn more about the magic here."

"Hnn..." She looks down at her feet, then flicks back up at me. "I have a room upstairs where you can sleep. I will go prepare some sheets for you."

CHAPTER FOUR

My body wakes me up at an ungodly hour. Not that I know what time it is, but darkness still blankets the snow outside the windowsill, and there's no noise coming from Kenjō outside this room. No matter how hard I try, I can't fall back asleep, so I take out my runes and try to bond. The first one I pull out of the bag is Uruz. I move my fingers over the carved symbol, and my mother's voice plays in my head almost as loud as if she were here with me.

My throat closes up, and I shut my eyes. I miss her so much.

The loud, eerie sound of an air raid siren makes me bolt out of bed. For a split second, I feel like I'm in the movie Silent Hill.

I swing the wool sheets off me, drop the leather pouch of runes on the bed to feel for my sweatshirt, pull it over my head, then cross the dark room Kenjō let me sleep in last night.

As I push the curtain she has in place for a door to the side, the overcast grey and dreary sky looms in from the top window of the tree house.

An eruption of wet coughing pours from downstairs over the sirens.

Down the spiral staircase, Kenjō is suited up and ready and rummaging through all her bottles, stashing away some while sticking herbs in a bag. She coughs some more into her hand as she flies through the forbidden curtain. Something crashes behind it, followed by the movement of boxes. I start making my way down.

She jumps back out of the curtain and closes it tight.

"Need any help?"

"No. We have to go now," she says with a raspy voice.

"What's going on? Are you feeling okay?"

"It happened again. The killings." Her voice sounds hasty, worried. "And yes, I'm fine. Just a cold."

I run down the rest of the steps and meet her on the first floor.

"When it happens, the Sword's Prefect calls everyone to the center of the town to investigate. You have to come too. If they find you here alone, they will take you in."

Ignoring for the moment the mention of there being a Sword's Prefect- whatever that is, I scan her living room full of what looks like a medieval set for Breaking Bad. Bottles full of all different color solutions display on a wooden shelf next to a table with ceramic mixing bowls, more clear bottles, and jars of herbs. "They search the homes?" Magic here is outlawed, and she makes potions. The way she just stashed stuff away tells me whatever she does here isn't minuscule or for personal use. It might be best that we go our separate ways; I don't want to get caught up in what she has going on. Drugs definitely lead to death. "Why would they take *me* in?"

"They expect everyone to be at the village center, and they will check. You will be a suspect if you don't go, è? Especially you."

"Why especially me?"

"The potion I gave you can be detected by other Ipani. Humans will not know the difference. Lucky for you, the Sword's Prefect is human. Remember, the potion is illegal. Besides, they won't be expecting a foreigner and might jump to the conclusion that you are the culprit." She moves closer to me, worry creasing her forehead. "You are not the culprit, are you?"

My lips part. "What? No."

"I believe you."

I grab my backpack. "We were going into town anyway, right? Let's go."

She turns to leave, and I follow her out the door, the biting wind chilling me as we climb down the ladder.

We sludge through the heavy snow to the narrow path we came in from, and I fall to step right behind her.

"Are murders like this frequent here?"

"No. They started fifteen days ago."

"With the way they check if everyone is present, how is it they haven't found the murderer yet?"

"There are rumors it's not an Ipani or Greek person killing people. But an animal."

Okay, now I'm confused. "What would lead people to think that? And then why would everyone be called as suspects?"

"By the way the bodies are left..." she pauses. "No one knows anything. It could be someone with a sick mind."

My eyes widen. That kind of serial killer, huh? Great timing to land here on my part. I don't need any run-ins with that guy or animal. I don't need to be put in the position for self-defense and get my family curse enacted on myself.

"Anyway, we do not go out at night. So if you are going to hang in the forest, be careful."

"Right, thanks for the warning."

We reach a clearing overlooking the village, and a whiff of a sea breeze reaches my nostrils. To the right of the village is a port with a few large ships on its dock. I hadn't given it much thought since I got here, but I'm wondering how large this place is.

"Hey, where are we exactly? Like, what's this place called?"

"This island is called Piupeki. But it is also known as Swords, since the time of the Empress."

I'm on an island. "How many islands are there?"

She jumps over a broken log on the path, and I swing my legs over it. "There are four main islands, with several smaller ones, not including Rutevenye, where the Empress lives."

"Why not include it?"

"Because it does not sit at sea."

I screw up my face.

After a moment of my silence, she finishes by saying, "It floats, è?" She points to the sky.

"Huh?"

"You do not have floating islands where you come from?"

"No...But this I'll have to see."

She doesn't say anything to that as we descend the steep hill we climbed yesterday. My shoes skid on ice, and I almost crash into her back.

"Watch it."

"Sorry, it's really icy."

"We're almost there."

Peering through the woodlands, I try to see the village. "You're kind of a recluse, aren't you?"

"What does that mean?"

"You like living far away from everyone?"

"Not me. My mother. Because of the potions I make, it's better that we are away from prying eyes."

"Family business, huh?" A smirk forms on my lips.

She ignores me and keeps trudging along through the snow.

"So, are you going to tell me?"

She glares over her shoulder but ignores me.

"That's alright, you don't have to. We just met."

"È? Tell you what?"

"What it is you're making in there. I saw you flying through the house, hiding herbs away."

"I told you. Magic is illegal here."

"Yeah, but I didn't know that was all you're doing. You could have been making herbal medicines or something."

She pauses, stares at me, parts her lips, then keeps going.

Right. So very illegal stuff.

We walk in silence the rest of the way until we get to tall city gates made of stone. The sirens keep playing as a line of people circle around the center of wooden buildings. As we near, dark spots taint the snow, and I assume it's mud from people's boots as they walk, but as we walk through the stone entryway, a bloody foot, black and blue, lies on the bottom of the stones.

Right.

In front.

Of the entrance.

My mouth drops, and I quickly close it as a man in armor scoops it up with a shovel and dumps it inside a wheelbarrow. I quickly cup my hand over my mouth and hold my breath. As the man spins the wheelbarrow around, I can't help but look inside it as we pass it by. The man pauses to wipe his disgruntled face.

Right inside is what I swear looks like a heart. A swollen, wet, and bloody heart. My eyes fixate on it, and I can swear I hear it still beating. But... that's impossible, right? How could it still be beating?

"Move along," the guard says.

My legs betray my eyes and move without me commanding them to.

Inside the village gates, the dark spots grow larger and redder. I swallow. That's not mud. It's blood. I follow the trail of red with my eyes to a body face down on the ground. A haunting moan comes from it, and I stiffen.

"Kenjō?"

She looks back at me.

"I'm confused," I say. "Was that a heart in that barrel?"

Her eyes are sorrowful as she gives me a single nod.

"Was there more than one death last night?"

"No, just him. Why?"

My brows knit together as I stare at the body on the ground, trying to listen for those low, heart-breaking cries.

Loud and clear, I hear them. Coming from that body, lying face down on the snow.

"Kenjō?" I ask again.

"Yes?"

"Was that heart still beating?"

"Of course, it was."

"Oh." I swallow. "Okay then."

A shrill cry erupts from a woman as she runs up to the body and throws her arms around him.

A man wearing metal armor approaches her, gently taps her on the shoulder, and attempts to pull her away. She screams, throwing her arms up and shoving him away.

Kenjō tugs on my sleeves. and I slowly put one foot in front of the other, trying my hardest to keep my eyes off the body.

I skim the crowd. Many of them look like Kenjō, with pointy ears. Some have stripes on their face, while others can't be seen through their clothes. There are also humans, the Ancient Greek descendants, I'm presuming.

Everyone is quiet and staring down at the ground. A mother shields her daughter's eyes as she guides her away from the center of the circle. The sound of our shoes crunching against the snow is the only noise that echoes through the air. Well, that and the sirens, I wish they'd shut off already.

Then I stop. A tall figure wearing a chrome, expressionless mask and black robes looms over the center of the circle, just above the body. His robe is held at his neck by a clasp in the shape of a shield, engraved with a sword over a yellow background. Where did he come from? He stands watch over everyone, his gaze stopping at me. I swallow.

An endless black void fills the holes where his eyes should be behind his mask. A chill runs down my spine.

Kenjō joins the line to the right, and I follow suit, trying to stay close, keeping my eyes on the figure.

"What is that?" I whisper to her.

"That's an Arcana soldier." She snaps. "Maybe it is best for you not to speak, è?"

I flick my gaze at her. "Why not?"

"Because you are a magician and a foreigner. Remember, the human Prefect won't be able to tell you are not from here, but Ipani can— the potion does not work on full Ipani, e! And someone might tell him."

My eyes widen. Even though she told me this before, the extent of it hadn't hit me.

A tall, lean human man wearing a gray wool hat hugging his head and a tight brown tunic barges through the crowd. More people come in through the gates and from the surrounding houses.

"Who is he?"

"That's Alec, the Sword's Prefect."

The sirens finally stop, and two men in armor close the gates, locking them as they clank shut. The only sound now is the sobbing coming from the woman hugging the corpse on the ground.

Her pained wails send an overwhelming sense of dread down to the pit of my stomach. It was only yesterday I buried my mother. My heart aches for this poor woman. I wish I wasn't here. I need to find that Ace of Swords, so I can get a portal open to save my aunt from my mother's fate. I can't afford to be stuck inside guarded city gates as a murder suspect with the rest of this village.

The masked figure starts moving toward the far end of the circle, standing in front of everyone.

"What's he doing?"

"They are now surveilling everyone, making sure everyone is here and accounted for."

"Except obviously the uh…" I nudge my chin at the guy on the ground. She shoots me a dirty look. "Sorry. So, who is he?"

"I don't know. I have not seen his face."

"She recognized him." I point to the weeping woman on the ground.

"Probably from his clothes."

The Prefect stands at the center, and everyone snaps their attention to him. "I want to know everyone's whereabouts and alibis from last night to this morning." He turns toward the woman crying over the body, then shoots a look to the two armed men who closed the gates. "Pull her away and bring the wheelbarrow."

My stomach turns. I remember what got put into that wheelbarrow.

The two men grab her from under her arms, lifting her as she kicks and screams. The one armored man who had approached her gently before now disappears to the side of a building. I rub my hands together as we wait for him to return.

The man comes back, pushing a wheelbarrow, and parks it next to the body. People gasp. Some hold their noses and look away.

"This morning," the Prefect starts, "my men scooped the

entrails of this young man off the snow." He reaches down, grabs the dead man's shoulder, and flips him to his back.

"Ugh," I cover my mouth with my hand. A gaping hole drops his innards onto a pool of blood on the snow. His jaw is gone. And I mean, ripped off. Trying to remain calm, I hold my breath.

The haunting moans emanate louder from the body. His chest is ripped to shreds, a gaping hole at its center where his heart was. Parts of his stomach are completely gone. Eaten, I presume.

Kenjō gasps.

I avert my eyes from the impossibly live corpse and shift my attention to Kenjō. "Are you okay?" I mutter. I knew there was a murder in town, but I was never expecting... this.

"No... I know him."

I gape at her. All the color has been drained from her face. "You do? ... Oh Kenjō... I'm so sorry. That's horrible."

She cups her face in her hands and squats down, staring at the mauled man. That had to be an animal. A human couldn't do that, right? What about an Ipani? I did notice they have double canines.

I squat down beside her. "Were you two close?"

"No, but he was my forager," she whispers.

"The guy you were coming here to meet today?"

"Yes."

Alec's footsteps crunch on the snow. "It is evident that this was done by some type of animal," he announces. "Rest assured, animal or oumala, we will hunt and kill it. We will make sure it pays."

The villagers start to clap, some cheer. A lady shouts across the circle and points at another woman a few feet away from me, "my neighbor told me this morning she saw a cat."

A few feet from her, an Ipani man dressed in a heavy burlap tunic laughs and shakes his head. "È? We will listen to the village crazy, now?"

The lady being pointed to nods furiously. Messy curls bounce over her eyes as she talks. "It is true. It was a large cat. I saw him with my own two eyes late last night."

"*Ts.*" Burlap dude rolls his eyes.

Ignoring the guy who just spoke, Alec circles around to her. "And what were you doing up late last night?"

"I heard a noise and wanted to check, nothing more."

"Was it a snow leopard?" Alec says.

"No, it was golden with spots."

The crowd begins to murmur, and Alec holds up a hand. "Impossible. Those don't come from Piupeki. If it's true, how would it have left Wands?"

"E!" A different Ipani man shouts. "What other kind of animal rips something to shreds? Cats play with their food."

An eyebrow arches high on Alec's face. "An āngaraeke could tear someone to shreds," he crosses his arms.

I tilt my head and whisper, "what's an anga—?"

"An āngaraeke is a Yeti," Kenjō whispers back. My nostrils flare. There are yetis here. And I'm meant to hike with a pocket knife up a mountain.

"It is probably a snow leopard," one of the guards shouts from the gates. "But if it is an unbound Ipani, we will find them, and they will pay the consequence."

"What if it's an oumala jaguar?" The lady who claimed to have spotted it says.

"This meeting is a waste of time." Burlap says. "It is obvious those pirates are behind this. No cat. *Ts.*"

I arch a brow at Kenjō. "Pirates?" I mouth.

A few people around the circle nod their heads. "I heard the *Devil's Gambit* was spotted nearing the docs two mornings ago. Those black sails with the horned skull can't be missed," burlap tells them, placing his arm behind his head. "*The Devil and his Undead Crew* are the only ones dastardly enough to want to destroy our village." He eyes Alec, who's standing with his arms crossed in front of him. "They mean to destroy the Empress and law-abiding villages, è?" He eyes everyone in the circle, one by one. "They will come and kill every last one of us, steal our cattle, and kidnap our children to join their crew."

A few women gasp. Others roll their eyes and laugh. A sinking feeling reaches my stomach. Pirates with a rebellious mission or a large cat. Great leads. I'm sure they'll find the murderer real soon.

Burlap snaps his gaze to me. "Laugh. But their crew could already be here among us. Pretending to be a visitor, è?"

Who me?

"The Arcana soldiers will find out soon enough," he says, his eyes fixed on mine. I stay quiet. I get it. These people don't get many visitors, and I stick out like a sore thumb with my North Face hiking clothes and blonde hair. The sooner I can get out of here, the better, but in the meantime, I don't plan on drawing any more attention to myself.

Alec shakes his hand. "Enough with the rumors. All ships are vetted. If it is true that oumala animals are being smuggled in, we would have to stop all ships from coming in—and we need supplies from Wands. My bet it is an āngaraeke, but we will take all measures to be sure. And capture the āngaraeke if it is one. As for any matters of piracy, all of our ports are secured, and there have been no such sightings of the Devil's Gambit nor his undead crew of miscreants." He says that last word like venom leaving his lips.

"What does oumala mean?" I ask Kenjō.

"Oumala are magical beings. Oumala animals, and oumala people. All Ipanis are born oumala until they are bound."

Oh, that's what she meant by being bound. Magic is the only thing that makes sense as to why this guy is somehow still alive. "So, your magic... was..."

"Taken from me at birth," she says. "All Ipani have to go through this because magic is dangerous."

"If you're born with it, isn't it messed up to strip people of their powers?"

She glances at me, her eyes wet, and a small smile curls on her face. Then it disappears. "Yes, many of us still believe that. But it is the law."

Looks like human fear is what conquered here.

I sigh. "I have to ask. Why is he still...why are his organs still..."

She stares at me and parts her lips. "It must be different for you in your world, è?"

"Umm... where I come from, people who are dead... are just dead."

"Then perhaps it is better if you do not know."

Fair enough.

The masked guard closes in where we are now. Wow, he works fast. Maybe this will be over soon, and I'll be able to go on my way.

"What are you going to do now?" I ask her.

"I don't know. This is a big problem for me. My mother is expecting a large batch of my potion. This will set her back by a lot if I do not have the plant I need."

"The rik—"

"Sh."

The Prefect claps his hands once. "But you will all still be questioned. You see... the young man had with him an illegal plant. Rikorō. Do you know of it?" A glint sparkles in his eye as he tilts his head sideways. His voice is jolly, but I can still detect sarcasm in it. He walks around, looking at everyone's faces. People in the circle shake their heads. I glance at Kenjō. Her features are stern, unreadable as she stares straight ahead.

"Whatever killed this man must have taken a large sum, but we confiscated the rest. I want to know what he was doing here with that dangerous, deadly plant."

"Deadly?" I look at her. Her frown deepens.

The masked soldier is at the person next to me now. I quickly stand upright, and so does Kenjō. The man next to me doesn't budge; he just looks back at the soldier. The soldier doesn't speak. He then shifts and walks in front of me.

I avert my eyes, trying not to stare at the void in his eye sockets.

The soldier steps closer, forcing me to look at him. His stature towers over me, and I glare deep into the eyes of his mask. I look for his eyes but don't find any. It really does go on forever in there. My nerves overcome me. Not knowing what to do, I extend my arm to shake his hand.

"What are you doing?" Kenjō asks.

"Trying to be polite," I say between my smile.

The soldier fixes his hollow smoky eyes on my wrist, revealing the Magician's mark. I quickly put my arm down, and his gaze lifts back to meet mine. His arms emerge from his sides and twist themselves into a white icy fog.

"Woah." I backpedal into a soldier behind me. Handcuffs emerge from the cold fog around my wrists, and the Arcana soldier spins around to face the Prefect who is making his way over.

I tug at my cuffs. "Hey, what's going on?"

Kenjō steps away from me. Her eyes frantically looking from me to the Prefect and the masked soldier.

The Prefect unsheathes a sword from his waist and points it at me. "Reveal your name, newcomer."

"I— uh..." How does he know I'm new? I hadn't spoken a word.

"I've not seen you here before. What is your business in Peki Guí?"

"I'm Harold Scott... And I'm just visiting?"

"Haroldscot? What kind of name is Haroldscot?"

"Just Harold is fine."

"Show me your wrist, newcomer."

Oh boy. I hold my wrists up, and he grabs them both by the linked chain, bringing them up to his nose. He gasps at the sight of my illegal roman numeral "I."

"Harodscot, by the Empress's court of Arcana, and her rule of The Tower, I hereby declare you under arrest."

CHAPTER FIVE

Two Arcana soldiers, with the same guise of black robes clasped with an emblem of a shield and a sword at the center, materialize in gusts of smoke on either side of the Prefect. I buckle back. The Prefect stands straight, glaring at me with his raised chin.

"W-wait." I have no idea what I'm going to say. "There's been a mistake."

"Search him for magical weapons," Alec says, ignoring my pleas.

Search me? Oh Frigg, my mother's runes. My chains jingle as I bring them down to pat my pants, momentarily forgetting I had cuffs on.

The guard behind me starts to pat my back with his gloved hands, making his way down the sides of my pants. After patting my ankles, he stops. I turn slightly to see him shaking his head. I stifle a sigh of relief. I left my mom's runes back at Kenjō's house. When the sirens went off, I grabbed my backpack and left. I must have assumed I stuck the runes back inside. I've never been so happy to forget something in my life.

"That does not mean he can't use ouma without a tool. Take him to the holding cell."

"No!" I yell. "I'm new here. I just got in yesterday." This can't be happening. Now my aunt really is going to die if I can't get out of this mess.

The Prefect lowers his eyes and puckers his lips. "Explain it to the Empress." He turns to leave.

"Ask Kenjō. I stayed with her last night," I blurt.

The Prefect pauses and spins on his heel, narrowing his eyes at me, then at Kenjō, who had been inching away slowly. Arching one brow, he says, "Surely, you are not harboring criminals, Kenjō? Demitri wouldn't be pleased to hear that, and it wouldn't take long for it to reach your mother."

I swallow. Did I just get her in trouble? I look around the circle. It's a small village and all. Kenjō shifts positions awkwardly, shooting me a dirty look.

"I'd hate to have to make that call, Kenjō; tell me the truth. Am I going to have to search your house?"

Kenjō blinks a few times but hides her expression. Not a bad poker face. She then raises her chin and takes a step toward us.

"No, I do not believe I have been harboring a criminal," she says.

"No?" Lowering his face to her, I hear him whisper, "you let a random man sleep in your house last night?"

My brow twitches. A man? Oh, he means me. Damn right, I'm a man.

Kenjō's cheeks redden as she stares back at Alec. "I found

him cold and alone near *Ruta Helāni.* He has not shown evidence of magic, and he needed help."

"Were you aware he has the mark of the Magician? Tell me you checked before bringing him into your home."

I stare at her, and she stares back at me. She could lie, and then I'd be taken in. She should lie, in all honesty. Why wouldn't she? She has her whole operation to hide, which he obviously doesn't know about since he's all bent over me being a "Magician" and threatening to search her home.

"Yes. I was aware," she says in a matter-of-fact tone. My jaw drops.

"Kenjō, what are you doing?" I whisper.

"And you still took him *in*?" He raises his tone in the last word. "What would Bronte say about this?"

"Leave my mother out of this. You and I both know we cannot fully understand the Empress's marks. Most importantly, Alec, he doesn't understand why he has it. Do you?"

"It does not matter whether we understand them or not, Kenjō. The law is the law. And Her Divinity would have my head if I were to ignore it." He sighs. "Look, I don't wish to ruin anyone's life, but it's the law."

"But there hasn't been a Magician in a long time, è?"

"What does that matter? There is one now, and he is here in front of us."

I stare at them both as they argue my case. Why does he care to listen? He doesn't seem like the type who would bend.

"He hasn't done any magic since he got here. At least not in front of me. Will you arrest someone because of a mark that may change overnight? Without a witness to his magic?"

"See? I told you I don't have magic," I say.

"That still doesn't explain why you have the mark of The Magician." Alec rubs his chin. "You might still become one."

"Is that enough to arrest someone and risk them enduring eternal suffering at the hands of the Empress?" Kenjō demands. "That's brutal, Alec, even for you."

"Even for me?" Alec turns to stare at her. "I just sent scouts to search for the beast killing our villagers. Other Prefects would be working on how it would benefit them." He hisses. "*Even for me,*" he rolls his eyes.

She scoffs.

Yeah, there was most definitely something between them.

"Let us speak privately," she tells him. Alec hardens his jaw and eyes me for a second.

"Watch him," he tells the soldier. I glance at the smoky eyes in front of me and swallow. Alec and Kenjō move away to the side and start whispering between themselves. My eyes wander around the circle of villagers, whose eyes are all on me, murmuring between themselves as they stare.

A few minutes later, Alec walks back to where I'm standing. "Uncuff him," he says between gritted teeth. The Arcana soldier taps on the chain, and both cuffs disappear from my wrists in a white fog.

I rotate my wrists. "Thank you for understanding," I say. "I promise I really don't know why I have this mark—"

"Where did you say you were from again?"

I part my lips to speak, but Kenjō passes me a look. Should I not say I came from another world?

"He's from Sotiria," she quickly states.

Alec raises his brows. "That is a long way from *Gā Pireson.*

I know nothing about healing plants, but Kenjō tells me you seek one that only grows in Pea Memoé."

I am? I glimpse at Kenjō, whose eyes widen as she purses her lips. Right, I guess I am. I'm assuming Gā Pireson is the Greek Temple ruins I landed in. "Yep, I'm off to find a healing plant."

Alec squints his eyes at me. "You are free to go, and you can thank her for that. But we will be keeping a close watch on you, Magician."

I nod.

The three Arcana soldiers back away and follow Alec to leave the circle.

"I urge you all to stay clear of the woods at night." Alec raises an arm toward the armed men at the closed gates, and they start to reopen the doors.

A few Ipani people—who I can tell are Ipani because of their subtly pointy ears and stripes, stop to stare at me. They mutter something to each other before cantering off.

"They can hear through the potion. You must go." I stare back at Kenjō, who is keeping her eye on the Arcana soldiers next to Alec.

"Do you think they'll tell?"

"Who knows. Be safe, è? You heard Alec." She flicks her gaze at me. "Whatever did this is still out there."

"Thanks for that. You didn't have to lie for me."

"I am not up for anyone being tortured if I can help it. But it was a close one for me too, è? Now, be off."

I give her a half smile. "Right, thanks for everything."

She nods. "Oh, one more thing."

"Yeah?"

"If you tell a Prefect you're from another world, they'll have no choice but to turn you into the Empress."

I smile. "Duly noted. Listen," As much as I hate to stick around, I need to go back for the runes. "I need to go back to your place. I left my mother's runes when we left in a hurry."

Agitation sprawls on her face, and her eyes roll to the sky. I quietly follow her out the village gates, passing by a group of Ipani girls who stare at me with confused looks on their faces.

"So, how could the Prefect understand me back there?" I break the silence. "I mean, I haven't given it too much thought, but now I'm wondering. Does the potion work both ways?"

"Obviously, or we wouldn't be able to understand you," She snaps.

I fall silent. The Ipani are the only ones who can tell I'm not from here. And she's half-Ipani.

We hike up the snowy mountain trail back to her tree house.

Okay, so my plan is to collect my things and then make it back down to the village, cross it without people asking me questions, and cross the woods that have just been closed at night. Then hike through the Eternal Mountains, or Pea Memoé, as they call it, and make it to some Greek Castle called Naó to find the magical sword that will help me open a portal. A long sigh escapes my lungs. I can do this. I scoff at myself. How? I have no idea, but if I don't, my aunt will die. And possibly so will I.

She sniffles in front of me.

"How are you feeling, by the way?"

She doesn't respond.

"You sound better at least, but you had a cold this morning..."

She looks over her shoulder at me. A tiny stream of blood leaves her nostril, and I pause. "Kenjō... you're bleeding."

"È?" She wipes the blood from her nose and gasps.

We stop by a nearby tree as she rummages for a cloth in her satchel. She wipes it away.

"Well, it doesn't look like you're still bleeding. Are you feeling okay?" I ask.

Her features soften at me. "Yes, I-I get altitude sickness, is all."

"Oh, yeah, I get it. That happens to me too. Are you going to be okay?"

A worried look spreads on her face momentarily. "Let's keep going. It is warmer at my home."

"Lead the way." I follow close behind, my legs falling into inches of snow. It must have snowed last night. I'm regretting the lack of clothes I brought with me. It would be nice to be able to dry these pants out before heading out again, but then again, they'll just get re-soaked. "So, what are you going to do now that your contact is... umm..." I lower my voice as if it somehow makes me sound more respectful. "Gone?"

"I don't know."

"How badly do you need that plant?"

"The Rikorō? Very badly. It is crucial to my ama's cause that I have it ready."

"Your second mother?" I smile. "See? I can remember Ipani words."

She hints at a smile, but her eyes are somber. "My biological mother died giving birth to me. My second mother was her wife."

"Oh. I'm sorry."

Memories of the burial resurface in my mind. A lump grows in my throat, so I stay quiet, letting her continue.

"My ama is a merchant. She is at sea right now. When she comes back, she will need the plant."

She lives up in these mountains all by herself. I clear the lump in my throat. "When does your mother dock?"

"It's hard to know. A few days tops."

"It's unfortunate what happened to your friend."

"Yes."

"What about your father? Is he around?"

She scrunches her features. "I never knew him. He was just a donor, è?"

"Understood." I rub my chin. "Do you know where the plant grows?"

"I do. But..."

"But?"

"It grows at the top of *Pea Memoé,* inside the cemetery of *Ahan Alēla,* the Haunted Forest. And I do not go there."

"Right. Too dangerous." I swallow.

"It is where my birth mother is buried," she says. "The haunted cemetery is where we bury our dead. Anyone close enough can hear the screams from their eternal torment."

Oh. I chew the inside of my cheek. Fun. "It makes sense why you don't want to go. I'm sorry."

"Besides, that beast is out there."

"Yeah, don't remind me."

She glances back and scrunches her nose. "You have magic, don't you?"

I give a solemn chuckle. "I'm not fully capable of using it yet. It was my mother's magic. I haven't bonded with them yet."

"But you have some. You can use it," She urges.

"I guess...Yeah, I do." I'll have time for bonding with them when I'm in the woods.

"You have protection, but you need practice, è?"

"Maybe. But, so do you, though, if you wanted to come along." I offer her a smile. What am I doing? She can't come with me. She's doing illegal stuff, and I've lost count of how many times she's lied. Which means, I have too. I'm guilty by association. What if this sets off my curse to be enacted already?

No. Frost would have formed at my eyes. I would have fallen already. I'm still okay. Besides, she knows this island. Would it be so bad if she came?

"I will not go into those woods."

"Not even with a handsome fellow like myself?" I show her my award-winning-grin. Even though I meant it as a joke, I sixty percent meant it.

She scoffs, and my grin evaporates.

When we reach the top of the mountain, the sun is now beaming in from the cliffside of her home. I start climbing the ladder after her, the snow is melted off, and the dark red wood is visible.

Inside, Kenjō unbuckles her fur coat and heads toward her stove to start taking out pots and pans. Keeping my jacket on since I'm heading out anyway, I take off my wet boots before I walk up the spiral staircase to find my bag and pouch of runes where I left them.

While I'm at it, I make the bed up, then slide my backpack over my shoulders. I grab my mother's runes, make sure the knot is held tightly around, and then stuff them in my pocket. It was stupid of me to leave them behind because I could have hiked miles by now, but I'm glad I did.

Glass shatters on the floor, preceded by a banging on a table and a grunt.

Yeah, time to go.

I make my way down the stairs, passing a disgruntled Kenjō who has her head rested on her hands on a table full of herbs and bottles. I would ask her what's wrong, but I'm sure it has to do with the plant she was supposed to get. Instead, I put on my shoes and head for the door.

"Well, thank you for your hospitality. I'll get out of your hair now."

She doesn't say anything, just stares down at her desk.

"Good luck," I finish, reaching for the door and pulling the handle.

"Wait."

I shut the door. "Yeah?"

She sighs and leans back on her chair. "The Ace of Swords is in the same area the Rikorō grows."

"The mountain you said you won't go to because—"

"I know what I said."

"So, does this mean you'll come?"

"I don't want to. And it will be dangerous with that beast out there, but..."

I slide my backpack off my shoulder.

"It looks like I have to."

"And you won't be alone."

She flicks her eyes to me. "I still do not know you. How do I know it is not unsafe to go with you?"

"I think if I was going to hurt you, I would have already, don't you think?"

She lowers her eye, "hn...You're right. We will be safer together."

"See? That's what I was talking about. We both need to go to the same place, so why not go together?"

"Fine."

"Yes!"

"But first, we need to prepare."

"Prepare? How?"

"You are not practiced enough to use your magic, so I need to create potion bombs just in case."

"Why would you need a bomb for? You seemed pretty good with a spear." There's also no way in hell I'm touching a bomb. That sounds like a curse-enacting cocktail.

She leans back on her chair and crosses her arms. "In case we need them against whoever is doing the killing."

CHAPTER SIX

I sit snug between two cushions on her wooden couch as she lights flames beneath small ceramic bowls and adds clear solutions mixed with green ones, drops at a time, from different glass bottles. Her hair is pulled back tightly behind her head, the tips of her ears pointing out through some messy strands.

I don't want to rush what she's doing, but I thought her getting this plant was urgent. I know my situation. Don't we have to travel on foot for a long time? I feel for my mother's runes in my pocket and take them out. Might as well use this time to bond. *Alright, runes, what can you tell me about this trip? Is there anything I need to know?*

A warm tingling feeling comes from one of them, and I pull it out.

Nauthiz.

Didn't I pull this one out when I was out in the cold? I pull out the journal from my bag and flip to the back.

Nauthiz emerges when there's a desperate need or urgency to do something. It screams the desperate need for a fire.

That was ironic the last time I pulled it out. But now, I feel like it's trying to tell me something. I stick the wooden rune back in the bag. *What do you mean?*

Again, a warm tingling sensation drifts between my fingertips, and I pull out another rune.

Uruz.

The wild ox. I chuckle. Wild and excited. I still don't agree it represents me. I try to keep a level head at the worst of times, so I don't fall privy to doing anything I'd regret. According to this journal, when the rune is reversed, it means death. My stomach twists in a knot, and I drop Uruz back in the bag and select another.

Raidho. The travel rune. Yes, I know I have to travel. Skimming the description next to it, my eyes fall on the words "spiritual journey." Are you trying to tell me I need to go alone again? The last time I pulled out the rune that meant danger coming my way. This is so confusing. I drop the rune in the pouch and lay my head back on the couch.

Kenjō looks over her shoulder, and I glance at her. She eyes the pouch of runes in my hand, then up at me. Frowning, she turns back to her work. Despite whatever illegal operation she and her mom have, she isn't so bad. She was nice enough to bring me—a total stranger—into her home and cover for me to the Prefect so I wouldn't be arrested in this strange land. Queasiness settles in my stomach. So far, my very existence here is illegal, but all this lying and covering up is bound to enact my curse.

But, given that I never made it to Jotunheim, my situation

could be far worse. As long as I don't get mixed up in whatever illegal stuff she's doing, I think I can travel with her to make sure I make it to the Ace of Swords.

The Ace of Swords requires a sacrifice. I haven't given much thought to what kind of sacrifice I'm going to have to make. My mind wanders to my aunt, frost covering her eyelids as she sleeps. Then to my mom's funeral, a heaviness presses on my chest. Whatever sacrifice I need to make, I'll do it. I need to get to Jotunheim to face the Frost Giants and resolve my family's curse.

I clear my throat. "How much longer is this going to take?"

"A few more hours," Kenjō says without looking up from her work.

My jaw slackens. "Hours? Uh... Don't we have to go?"

She sets her stirring utensil down on the table and turns to me. "It is better if we go tomorrow. We'll want to leave early enough to get a head start so that we are not traversing into the woods late at night. I don't want to be stopped going in, and I'd like enough time to find a safe enough place to make camp before nightfall."

Well, if she's going to be logical... It looks like I'm stuck here another night. "Okay then, Doc, do you need any help?"

She narrows her eyes at me. "Doc?"

"You're the one who seems to have the answers."

She looks at me quizzically, then turns back to her potion making, picking up her stirring utensil. "No, you don't know how to do this."

"Well, why don't you show me?" Is there any harm in making the explosives as long as I don't use them? I just want to speed up the process.

She sets down her utensil again and arches her head back. "This takes a long time to learn."

"You don't have to teach me everything," I stand, "just tell me what you're doing so that I can help you make them."

"I guess it will make the process go by faster."

"That's the spirit. Where do I start?" The idea of learning how to mix magical potions sends a sudden burst of excitement through my chest. A buzzing comes from my mother's runes, and I pause. Queasiness settles in my stomach. Maybe this is wrong. I reach into the bag and pull out a rune; my chest tightens as Kenaz feels heavy in my hands.

The one that represents my mom. Given that it means the flame of knowledge, I don't think it's trying to warn me at all. It wants me to learn. Or my mom does.

Kenjō stands and grabs a small ceramic pot and candle, identical to the one she's working with, and sets it on the far side of the table, where there's a wooden chair. I take a seat and watch as she pulls out another stir from a drawer to her left and hands it to me. As I take it from her, her mark shows on her wrist, and I'm suddenly distracted away from the runes.

Why am I the Magician?

Her mark is so much more extravagant than mine. Five swords spanning out like a fan. Five swords. What does that mean? It's definitely part of the Minor Arcana, and I only know that because my aunt has a deck of tarot cards back home. Not that she ever uses them, but she feels it's good to have a general knowledge of other forms of magic. Turns out she's right. The Magician is part of the major arcana. Too bad mine is outlawed.

"Are you ready?"

"Hm?"

She locks eyes with me. "What are you staring at?"

"Oh, sorry. I was just wondering... since you make magical potions, how come you don't have the Magician's mark?" I raise up my wrist.

She shakes her head as she grabs a bottle with a neon green solution. "Many have spent their lives studying these marks to conclude that nothing is conclusive. The only thing I can say is that I have not had my ouma since I was bound. So maybe, a Magician has it inside of them. It doesn't matter if I make it externally."

"I'm sorry they did that to you."

"Why? It is our life here."

"Still. Nobody should be deprived of who they are."

She stops to gaze at me for a second, and I swear I can almost see her blushing. I clear my throat. "So, where do we start?"

"Yes, this lime green solution is called *itanchi*, and this blue one is called *buchiveru*, it is a stabilizer to keep it stable until impact, è? So be careful handling it."

"You got it, Professor."

"È?"

"Because you're teaching me things..."

She grimaces, and I chuckle. "Relax, I'm only teasing." I carefully pick up the lime green solution and twist it in my hands. "So, this will make stuff go boom?"

"Yes. But there's another one that we also need to make." She leans across the table and picks up a light blue solution. I better get those memorized.

"What does it do?"

A mischievous smirk peeks on the corner of her lips, and her eyes narrow at the bottle. Oh, now this side I haven't seen yet.

She stands up from her desk and heads toward the door. "Follow me."

"Where are we going?"

She bounces the glass bottle in her hand, and my eyes widen. "Are you scared?"

"Me?" I scoff and push myself up off the table.

Outside, a lot of the snow has melted from the ground.

"Stand there," she points to the ground beside the tree she had tied me up to. When I hesitate, she grabs my arm and pulls me.

"Can you blame me? I don't know what you're up to."

"I'm not tying you up. Stand still."

I do as she says, readying myself this time, just in case she decides to change her mind. She backs up a few paces.

"Run at me," she says.

"You want me to run at you?"

"Yes, charge."

"Oh no, that's okay. I think I'll stay right here where you told me to stand. I'm good."

"What's wrong with you? I'm telling you to attack me."

"Yeah," I scratch the back of my head. "I saw your ninja moves. I don't know what you're planning, but I know it isn't good."

"You're scared."

"Really, I'm not. I have moves of my own. I just... don't want to fight right now."

She scowls at me, turns to a lump of snow in the ground,

bends over, places her bottle on the ground and proceeds to pack some snow into her palm.

"Kenjō, what are you doing?"

The evilest smirk in the history of smirks slides on her face. "Kenjō, no. Don't you dare thro—"

A snowball crashes against my cheek so hard that I almost lose balance. "Ow." I rub my cheek. Why did that have to be so hard? Kenjō chuckles and picks up her bottle from the ground.

"Come at me."

I wipe the cold, wet snow off my face. "Fine." She wants me to charge at her. She asked for it. I position myself into a running stance and leap into a sprint. Just before reaching her, Kenjō sidesteps, arches her arm, and throws the glass bottle hard on a rock next to my feet. I almost stumble over myself as a blue light flashes in my eyes, followed by a blue gas.

I spin around and see no sign of Kenjō. The ground tilts beneath my feet, and the world spins around me. I clutch my stomach and fall to my knees.

"W-what d-did you d-do?"

Seconds later, Kenjō is pulling me away and leaning me against the tree.

"I'm sorry. Are you alright? I didn't think it would be that strong."

Two images of her face sway in front of me, and I slowly blink them into one. "What happened?"

She sits up. "That was my invention."

I prop myself up on my elbows, despite my head feeling like it weighs fifty pounds.

"I call it Smokey. No one knows how to make this but me, the perfect element of surprise."

"Well, it definitely surprised me," I say glumly.

"I am sorry, Harold. I meant only to disorient you. Not knock you out."

"Yeah, just how did you disappear so fast?"

"I didn't. That's part of the ouma." As Kenjō talks about the process of mixing plants I've never heard of in a magical equation I can't possibly imagine, I pretend to follow. The soft reflective glow from the melting snow shines on her skin. Her eyes light up as she describes her invention, and I can't help but think she looks like some sort of elven angel. Alarmingly beautiful. Unique in every way. My head hits the ground flat.

"Harold?"

"Yep." I sit up again. "Sorry, head hurts."

"Let's go inside, è?"

"Good idea. Let's make more... what did you call it? Smokey?"

"Yes, Smokey."

Back inside, she pulls out the ingredients we need to make the two solutions she wants to take with us. The death bombs and the smoke screen bombs. At least that's what I'm calling them. Pushing my queasiness at bay (which I'm noting comes up whenever I'm afraid of enacting my curse, I swear this mysterious hot crime lord is gonna get me killed), we work without stopping far past lunchtime. She teaches me about the different plants we're working with and their oumala properties.

Oumala is a magical organism from this world-one that is connected with the Aō, at least she tried to explain. From what I understand, it's a dimensional plane we can't see with our naked eyes, but some animals are able to disappear into it and reappear like the Cheshire cat. Not that she knows who the Cheshire cat is, but it's how I understand it. That, I'd like to see.

And ouma just means the magic itself.

I slowly stir the contents of the catalyst into the explosive solution.

"You are doing good."

Careful not to move too quickly as this needs to be stirred with care, I give her a smile and nod. I've only known her for a minute, but there's something about her that calls my attention. She's... serious and devoted to her work. Protective and wicked smart. But there's also a hint of playfulness that's dying to get out when she looks at me.

"Let's take a break."

I put down the stir. "Really? I'm starving."

"I haven't been hungry all day. I tend to zone into my work." She pushes off her seat and disappears behind a red curtain next to her stove. Minutes later, she comes out with bread and a jar of what looks like butter. "I will cook some more rabbit, è?"

"Sounds good. Can I help?"

She sets the bread and jar on a separate table near the couch, and I switch seats. We obviously do not want to eat near explosives. She moves her hair from her face and smiles.

"If you want."

A trickle of blood leaves her nose.

"Kenjō? Your nose is bleeding again..."

She gasps and runs back through the curtain.

I hope to Odin this isn't going to be a problem in the woods.

CHAPTER SEVEN

THIS TIME, WHEN I WAKE UP AT THE CRACK OF DAWN, I reach for my runes and stuff them securely in my pocket. When ready, I head down the spiral stairs to meet a fully equipped Kenjō, ready to go. Her spear is strapped to her back like she's ready for war, as she ties a large leather satchel shut. God, she's hot.

She glances up at me and catches me staring at her. She moves a strand of hair behind her ear. "There is fresh fruit on the table if you are hungry," she says.

"Thanks." Hiding my burning cheeks, I skip over to the table next to the stove burner and grab an apple. "I slept like a log last night. A snowstorm could have passed through, and I wouldn't have known about it." I take a bite of the apple. "Are you feeling better? Any more nosebleeds?"

"No, I'm fine. Let's go." Grabbing onto her leather satchel, she swings it over her head so that it crosses her chest, and we head for the door.

Airstrike sirens blare through the air and we pause to stare at each other. "Again?"

"Oh no... we don't have time for this." She jumps down her tree house and lands on her feet.

I scurry down the ladder behind her. Yeah, I'll prove my suaveness later. I won't land as flawless if I copy her right now. You know, my legs are still waking up.

We walk briskly down the snowy mountain path, out to the village.

Once there, the line of villagers who live on the perimeter of the city gates silently form a circle. The sun hasn't even risen yet and Alec is already at the forefront, with bags under his eyes. They must have been hunting the beast all night.

He's speaking privately with a tall, dark-skinned man wearing what looks like a smaller version of a bishop's hat on top of short-clipper hair, black and round but with a pointy top. He has on a turtleneck black robe and pants. A gold clasp similar to the Arcana soldiers decorates the top of his turtleneck.

Alec's eyes skim over to us and pause. Bishop-looking dude stops to stare at us as well.

"Who's that?" I mutter under my breath.

Kenjō hesitates and then proceeds toward him. "That's Demitri. He's friends with my mom, but he's the Empress's advisor."

The Empress' advisor. I stare at him, and his beady eyes move between me and Kenjō. He curls his lips up at me in distaste but then softens his features to greet Kenjō. Oh, we're off to a great start.

"What happened?" She asks them as we meet them. I stand

face to face with Demitri. One of the Arcana soldiers appears to stand close behind him and now I have two creepy dudes staring at me. Three if you count Alec.

"Get in the circle, Kenjō." He moves over to me. "Harodscot, have you found your plant yet?"

I square my jaw. "No." I bite down the queasy feeling over lying about what I'm really doing here. "And it's just Harold."

A few Ipani pass us by and Kenjō shoots me a dirty look.

She leans into Alec, and he furrows his brows. "That is what I came to talk to you about. I am going to voyage into the forest with Harold."

"Mmmm... Kenjō, I don't think that is a good idea. I have banned entry to these woods at night."

"Why would you be going into the woods?" Demitri asks curtly. "And you haven't introduced me to your friend yet." He turns to me. "I want to hear more about this Magician everyone is talking about."

He gives me a hard stare and I narrow my eyes at him. What do I tell him? If he's the Empress's advisor, I wonder if Alec called him here because of me. My eyes fall to the emblem decorating his clasp. It's of a curved spider-web, the Empress's symbol no doubt, as he's her advisor.

"He's from Sotiria," Kenjō quickly lies. "I'm helping him find a healing plant he needs. And in return..." she lowers his voice to Demitri, "he's going to help me with a plant that I need. You know, the mountain can be dangerous. He has...skills."

Alec screws up his face. Demitri stares blankly at her, then raises an eyebrow at me. Something tells me he isn't buying her lies and that makes my stomach hurt even more.

"Entry is banned at night," she repeats. "But if we leave now, we can make it back before then. And if not, we can make it to the other side before nightfall."

"You want to skip this meeting so that you can get a head start," Alec says.

Kenjō nods, "Yes."

He looks from her to me, then back toward the center of the village square. Bloody entrails are spread throughout the frosted ground. It didn't appear to snow last night, so as I squint I recognize body parts mixed with mud, making it look like something like pulled pork. My stomach turns. Whatever this thing is, it definitely likes to play with its food.

Alec returns his gaze to us. "I cannot allow it. Look at what the beast did to a dear neighbor."

Demitri holds up his hand, silencing Alec. He stares at me. "Why should we allow a Magician to roam around the woods anyhow? And with my precious Kenjō no less." He turns to her. "Your mother would have all our heads. Well, Alec's at least. She wouldn't be able to take mine."

My heart thuds in my chest. He's never going to let us go. Forget finding a sword or a way out of here, I'm about to end up in some jail somewhere.

"Nonetheless, I will allow it," he says. "But you must go in haste." I do a double-take. What?

Alec's eyes widen. "But Hierophant, are you sure that's wise? You said yourself he's a M—"

Hierophant. I wish I had brought a guidebook on the tarot.

"I trust Kenjō knows what she's doing and if she has reason to go into the woods, then we should trust her." he smiles curtly at her. My brows furrow. This isn't making sense to me, but I'd be foolish to question him out loud and ruin our chances of going.

"Hierophant, you can't be serious..." Alec says. "It's far too dangerous, what if the beast catches up with her? She'll be all alone out there."

"Are you questioning my authority, Prefect?"

Alec snaps his mouth shut. A moment later he turns to Kenjō, "I can send a hunter with you—" he arches his back and raises his arm, calling one of the guard's attention. The armed man starts to move toward us.

Kenjō shifts uncomfortably and Demitri intercepts again.

"That won't be necessary," he quickly adds. "She won't be alone, and two people can move faster than three. Adding a third might slow them down. Isn't that right, Magician?" His eyes bore into mine. What's his end game here?

Demitri takes a step uncomfortably close to my face and lowers his voice, his pointy nose almost touching mine. "But do not mistake my generosity for recklessness. I will have scouts on you at all times."

I gulp.

Alec brings his arm down, and the guard stays put, confusion on his face. "Very well, be careful. I don't want your mother after my head if she finds out her precious daughter has been shredded to bits."

"I will."

Alec flicks his gaze to me. "And you, Jost-harod."

Odin's balls.

"As the Hierophant says, that doesn't mean we won't be keeping watch on you. The Empress has eyes everywhere."

I raise my hands. "You got it."

Alec quirks a brow, then turns back to the circle nearly finished forming. "Safe travels."

Kenjō nods once and we're on our way. I resist the urge to look back at the Hierophant, who I'm sure has his beady eyes glued to me.

We sludge on the muddy snow along the village walls that lead to the forest entrance.

As the forest comes closer into view, I gaze into the dark twisted pathway and wonder if uniting our journey is a good idea. I still have no idea what I'm getting myself into. And even though Kenjō has proven to not be murderous--I've forgiven her tying me to a tree due to her not knowing me either, she's just a girl my age. A strong, trained, Ipani girl. But how much experience could she have? Especially since she's already said she doesn't go into these woods.

I reach into my pocket and take out a rune. I don't even bother to ask a question; they should feel my fear. I hold the rune up to my face.

Isa. Ice.

Is it telling me to stop? To not go into this forest? Or warning me of my family's curse?

"E!"

"What?" I stick the rune back in my pocket.

She grabs my arm as if trying to shove it deeper into my pocket. "Do not use your magic here. You heard Alec. They are watching."

"Oh yeah, sorry...Let's keep going."

I'm probably confused by what the runes are trying to tell me because I haven't bonded with them. And the only way to bond is to keep using them.

She turns to face the beaten path of the forest. Worry lines crease her forehead and I gulp. She raises her chin in a show of courage and carries onward.

"Hey, what was with the Hierophant anyway? Why did he let us go?" I've been waiting to be far enough away to ask her that.

"We were lucky he was there. He is the Empress's advisor, but he is friends with my mom, è? He has a soft spot for us Ipani and has known me since I was a baby. He's always let me do what I asked."

"So, you've just got the Empress's advisor wrapped around your pretty little finger, don't you?" I smirk.

She casts me a confused look, but I keep smiling.

Don't worry Aunt Liv, I'll get to Jotunheim, and break our family's curse soon enough.

Once we're past the invisible line of the entrance, the air feels crisper. My boots squeak as I make heavy footprints on the untouched blanket of snow.

The leafless trees are covered in glistening white, and there doesn't seem to be any other life apart from us. We walk in silence, only the sounds of our boots and coats chafing. So I do the only thing I do when I'm feeling awkward. I talk.

"Are we in those woods yet? The cemetery ones..."

"No. We have a long hike before we get there."

"Do you really think we'll be back before the day ends?"

She scoffs. "I only told him that so he'd let us go."

"Ah. So, what's the deal between you two anyway?"

"È? What do you mean?"

"He seems.... Friendly to you. And he's the Prefect. He didn't seem so friendly to anybody else." Especially not me.

"He isn't so bad; he follows the rules. He only means to protect the village."

"But?"

She shrugs. "But nothing."

"You two have a history, don't you?"

"A history?"

Maybe that didn't translate well. "Were you two ever... together?"

She grows silent.

"Sorry, that was a personal question."

"Sort of, but not really," she says.

"Oh?"

"He's too good."

"Oh yeah? That bad, huh?"

She chuckles. "He doesn't know about my mother's business dealings. I cannot involve myself with him."

"Wow, this stuff with your mom really has you tied up."

She stops and faces me, her hair whips around her face. "What she does, is more than just a crime business, è?"

"...Okay."

Her eyes harden. "It is for the good of our kind."

"Got it." It sounds like she's trying to say the ends justify the means in whatever they're doing, but I don't know her well enough to say that. I'm better off staying in my lane.

She studies my face for a second then continues walking.

"Eh, don't put him on such a high pedestal," I say after her.

"I do not know what that means."

"What I mean is, he probably isn't all that."

She quirks a brow at me.

"I mean, the guy can't even get my name right. What? Is he hard of hearing?"

She scoffs, but then a smile spreads on her face. She stops and trails to the left and I almost bump into her back.

"Kenjō?"

"Look over here." She points down to a plant near the base of a tree, a few feet into the beaten path. "This plant is called Buchiveru, it was the catalyst plant we used to make these bombs." She grabs it from its base and pulls it clean out, sticking it into her satchel.

I squat down to take a look at another that was just beside it. It has a thick stem, with minuscule blue follicles, all the way up to a green flower, with blue edges. "It's pretty."

"It's actually a vine," she says. "It will eventually grow to wrap around this tree." She places her hand on the bark and looks up. I do the same. "Most people only use this plant as a catalyst, but I discovered, when mixed with the same plant but male, it creates a hallucinogenic gas."

"Are you talking about the smoke bomb you knocked me out with?"

"Yes. Different doses can cause different effects." She bends over and grabs the one I was looking at."

"That's awesome," I say.

"It's a great plant, underrated."

"No, I mean, I think it's awesome that you know so much about plants."

Her cheeks redden and she turns to reach the trail.

"So, how do you make that potion you gave me yesterday? The translation one."

"Unfortunately, that one only grows in Sāgirang."

"Where?"

"It is also called the Isle of Wands. But us natives against the changes still call it by its original name, *Sāgirang*."

Wands. And this is Swords. From the Tarot. "And where is Wands?"

"Far away on another island. It takes about a month to travel by ship."

I whistle. "Have you ever been there?"

She shakes her head. "I have never left Piupeki."

"Oh wow. So, how long does this translation potion last?"

"Not long? I don't know, it should last you a few days. Indakepoa is a slow-acting plant but I didn't have that much, so it's hard to say."

I chew my bottom lip. Okay, that's not good.

"That's another reason why you need to hurry, Harold, è?" She gives me a playful smile, but I don't find it funny.

"Well, maybe you can teach me some Ipani, then, eh?"

"Hn." She smiles back, her little fangs pressed against her bottom lip. "Or Imboe. Either way, someone will hear your otherworldly accent and will start asking questions."

"And then they'll for sure know I'm a Magician and send me to the Empress."

"Yes."

Beautiful. "So, let me guess. The other islands are called... Cups and Pentacles?"

"How did you know?"

"Lucky guess. We have the Tarot where I come from too."

"But you said you don't get marks."

"That's right. What I said was true. They're just cards to tell divination. Nothing like here."

"I wish I lived there, then," she says.

"That would be interesting." What would happen? Would we have to hide her ears? And her stripes? How would humans on earth react?

"There is a legend of our ancestors here in Piupeki."

Light snow starts to fall over the soft morning light.

"I love stories," I fall into step beside her so I can hear her better.

"It isn't a story. I tell you this because where we are going, there will be more ruins, but this time, Ipani ruins."

"What were they before?"

"Ipani forgers of weapons, who had a special ouma that could bend steel at their will. The steel in Piupeki is alive, it is special, and only they had the bond to make them."

My brows raise. "Wow. Are these weapons still around?"

"No, during the Ipani and Greek wars, around one hundred years ago, they were all destroyed, as were the ancients. Only one sword remains, inside *Naó*, the Helāni temple I told you about."

"Is that the Ace of Swords?"

"They say it was closely tied with the Aō, but as it mixed with the Empress's Halani magic, it became imbued in a card."

I take that in as we walk up what's becoming a steep hill.

"Anyway, I tell you this so that you understand Pea Memoé, that cemetery we will cross, expands across the perimeter. It is guarded by the spirits that haunt the forest."

Her right hand is clutched tightly around the strap of her leather satchel, her arm rigid with tension.

Spirits that haunt the forest. I'm not afraid of ghosts but I can tell she is. Good thing she has me to keep her safe then. "So, about this sacrifice. Are there any legends saying what type, and if it's been done before?"

"I don't know of any legend, but I do know not anyone can pick up the sword. Some believe that with the proper ouma, or magic, they could pick it up."

"Kind of like Excalibur?"

"Who is that?"

"Nevermind."

"They say it would not be an Ipani's ouma that could do it... Not that there are any unbound Ipani left in Piupeki..."

"Like I said, I haven't bonded with my magic yet. How am I meant to pick up the sword if a sacrifice isn't enough, and my magic isn't working?"

Kenjō glances at me from the corner of her eye. "Be optimistic, è? You have a few days to bond with your magic, so long as no one is watching. Don't give up hope. One thing they say about the Ace of Swords is that it will only help someone true of heart. That is why I suggested you find it."

"I guess I have a lot of bonding to do with these runes on this trip." The sunlight reflects on the metal of her arrowhead through the trees as I follow her up the path. Despite the frigid temperature, the sunlight coming in sends a nice warmth as we walk off the cold.

"Ipani people have to make a connection with their ouma as well. Whatever it may be, they need to learn to bond with that spirit, be it of the forest, or the snow, or animals even." She points to the forest and snow around us as she speaks. "Not that I will ever know."

"It was taken from you at birth, right?"

"Yes."

I stay quiet, listening to the sound our feet make on the snow. A few birds sing on the trees above us, and I glance up at the silver glistening branches but don't see where they're coming from.

"There is a rumor that says if anyone were to collect all the ace cards, they could wield power over the Empress. But it seems like lore, and impossible, no one in Ipa has a pure heart, and I heard a few of the Aces cannot be touched by human or Ipani."

I chuckle. "Just like I thought portals to different dimensions were impossible."

"That's true."

As we hike up this mountain, the number of trees starts to lessen and I can see a clearing up ahead. Clouds move over the sun and grey skies make way through the scarcity of the pines. She sludges to her right, stepping over some deep piles of snow and I pause and glance toward the cleared pathway.

"Kenjō? Are you sure you want to go that way? It looks easier over there."

"Do you want to let Rutavenye know we're walking?"

"What's Rutavenye, and what does it matter if we're walking?"

"Rutavenye is the floating island, where the Empress lives. And it matters in case they do checks. They might not, but I can't take a chance. I need to get this over with."

I'm still stuck on "floating island." I almost forgot about that little detail she told me about yesterday. I take a few steps out toward the clearing and Kenjō runs behind me, grabbing onto my jacket.

She points to the sky, and I look up.

"You can't see it from here, Harold. But we can see it from the highest peak."

"You're joking." I turn back to the clearing. "I really want to see a floating island."

"You really have never seen one before?"

I laugh, "No."

She purses her lips together and drops her shoulders. "Okay, only for a little, then we stick to our path."

"Promise."

She takes the lead and I follow close behind, with a pep in my step. I wish I could take a picture. I chuckle to myself—it's not like cell phones can work in different dimensions. Maybe I can draw it. It's not the same though.

A loud whistling sound falls from the sky.

Kenjō holds her hand out and I stop.

A fuming, long gust of white icy smoke lands in front of us, followed by another. Arcana soldiers in black robes and chrome masks stare dead and center at us on the trail.

Another whistling sound comes down. It sounds like bombs are being launched at us.

I duck as one lands behind me, I spin around, now back-to-back with Kenjō.

Its dark smoke-filled hollow sockets of the mask bore into me and all I can feel is an overwhelming sense of dread.

CHAPTER EIGHT

"Don't move," Kenjō mutters behind me.

The masked soldier glides in closer and if I budge, I might brush their mask with my nose. "Wasn't planning on it but this might be a good time for you to throw one of those harmless getaway bombs?"

"That's a bad idea. There are soldiers in the clearing now. We are surrounded with nowhere to run."

Oh, joy.

More soldiers land in the woods in front of me, as well as to the sides. "What do we do?" I whisper through the corner of my lips. "This guard is trying to peer into my soul or something."

"The others don't seem to be staring at us."

I dare turn my gaze away from the soldier staring me down and look toward the trees. "They look like they're searching for something." I stare back at the chrome reflective mask who has now turned his attention to my wrists. I turn my right wrist slightly inward, concealing my magician's mark. Can they tell without seeing it?

Yesterday, at the village, the masked soldier seemed to pause on me, suspecting something strange. Maybe it was just because he didn't recognize me as one of the villagers.

The soldier glides back and I let out a sigh of relief.

"They must be hunting the beast that is killing villagers. But they recognize your mark, so you are of interest to them," she says.

"Ah, I'm the lucky one."

"And most likely Demitri told them to keep an eye on you."

I will have scouts on you at all times.

A shiver runs down my spine. "Right."

We both relax and step away from having our backs pressed against each other. We glance around, in case any of them decide to come back.

"Just so I'm clear, they're not psychic or anything, right? That's not a thing here?"

"It depends on what their ouma was before the Empress imprisoned them to serve their life as her army. These have the ouma of ice. The ones in her Tower *are* psychic, I'm afraid."

Why do I have to be right?

She takes a stride toward the clearing, and I rush after her.

"I thought you didn't want to go that way. I can see the floating island later if it's safer to go through the trees."

"Not anymore. I don't want to be walking side by side with the soldiers in thick woodland."

That's a good point.

We step on heavy snow mounds as we proceed to the top of

the mountain, reaching the open space at the peak. My chest tightens as cold air enters my lungs and I cup my palms over my nose. Along our left is a long, dry stone wall, that extends as far as my eyes can see.

One lonely soldier surveys the area and stops to gaze at us. It glides over to us to inspect us, stopping at me first.

Yay.

He levels with me; I try to squint through the black smoke swirls that is his eyes. Is anything in there? Kenjō said they were prisoners? Where are their eyes? Why can't we see them?

He circles around me and then comes out to Kenjō's other side. She clutches her travel bag as it leans forward as if sniffing the air around her. Then it stops at her face, and inches forward.

Blood drains from my face as Kenjō's eyes widen. Does it smell the potions in her bag? Illegal activity always means death for my family. Hanging out with her is going to enact my curse. Despite the cold, sweat trickles down the back of my neck.

An air horn blows in the distance and the soldier looks up. Its expressionless features staring off into the trees, then upward behind him. In a swirl of white smoke, it disappears.

Kenjō drops her shoulders.

"That was close. Do you think it was smelling your potions?"

"I think so."

"Why do you think they were called back?"

She gives a modest shoulder shrug and then points out toward the sky. "Look."

I squint to where the sun is shining to our right, trying to see what she's pointing at. "I don't see anything."

"Come closer then."

We walk a few paces and I shield my eyes from the sun. A few clouds slowly move away, revealing a large mass of rock, sure enough floating by itself in the sky. Woah.

"That is Rutavenye," she says. "It means floating rock. It is where The Tower is."

"Rutavenye," I repeat. "That's a great description for it. So, the Empress lives there?"

"Yes." She turns to keep walking out toward the horizon and I follow, my boots squeaking on the thick snow. "A few years ago, one of the Arcana soldiers came down here and melted a frozen wall with their mind."

"With their mind?"

"Technically with their ouma, è? But from afar it looked like they were using their mind."

"So, they still have their magic. Or some of them do?"

"Not exactly. The Empress takes away their ability to make choices, speak, and use their ouma when they want and how they want it."

"So, they're like puppets and the Empress is their puppeteer."

"If the Empress decides we need magic down here that she won't or can't do herself, she will send a soldier to do it, but they have no ability to use it any other way."

"What kind of magic does the Empress have?"

She bites her lip. "Do you remember the dead man from yesterday, whose heart was still beating, and you were confused..."

My breath escapes me. I nod. That is one image that will haunt my nightmares.

"We are all told from young, she holds dominion over the card of Death. She knows who dies, and she controls our end." Her voice quivers and I reach for her arm, but she turns away. "For some reason unknown to anyone, she stops our bodies from joining soil, and prevents us from rejoining the Aō. We are left to suffer, endlessly, forever.

"Yeesh, that's grim."

She shudders a breath. "Come on, we won't make it to the next wooded area until evening at this pace. When we get there, we should make camp."

It's a long stretch walking along the side of a stone wall toward the next wooded area, just beyond the horizon.

I know they're only looking for the beast who is killing off their villagers, and that's a good thing. But I can't shake off the feeling of how they keep staring into me. Like they're expecting me to pull a rabbit out of a hat. I guess Demitri is making good on his promise to always be watching me. If anything, he's only trying to keep Kenjō safe.

I have no idea what time it is, or even how they measure time here, but it feels like it would be around four or five o'clock. Seeing as how it's a snowy island, the sun is already beginning to set. The snow crunches beneath our feet as we hike.

"Do you think we're far enough away from the beast at this point?" I ask.

"We should be, I hope. This is why I wanted to make it past those woods."

"We made good time; I think."

"Yes. And there is still some light out, so we can keep walking until we reach that frozen stream." She points over to her right. "Otherwise, we would have to hunt. But there is fish in that water."

"What would we be hunting?" I ask.

"Common rabbit."

"Why is it common?"

"It is not oumala. The only ones who eat those are some humans."

"Well, not this human," I say, not that I exactly understand what an oumala animal does differently.

"Oumala animals can go inside the Aō anyway, so hunting them is not easy."

"That's good, isn't it?"

"One thing I regret about being bound is I will never understand the bond between an Ipani and their familiar."

"What kind of bond would it be?"

"Some Ipani can share a special connection with an oumala animal. It is something I always dreamed of having."

I grow quiet as we close the distance between the clearing and the next woods. My aunt's crow comes to mind. I wonder if Snorri would be considered oumala here. Kenjō quickens her pace, so my strides grow longer. Funny she doesn't even use a map.

"Kenjō, if you've never been out here, how do you know where to go?"

"I know where my mother is buried. I've always known."

"Sorry."

She deviates from our path and starts toward the frozen stream.

"Have you ever done this before?" I ask her.

"Plenty of times." She takes off her satchel and unstraps her spear. "Watch and learn."

I hide a smirk. Leaning over the edge, she holds her spear in her right hand and stabs the ice. A ripping crack bursts from below and a stream of flowing water emerges through the ice. I inch close behind her, afraid to step too near the edge and fall in. Diving into freezing water is not on my agenda today.

She digs back into her satchel and pulls out a rope, swiftly tying a knot. This girl is nifty. Just as I think she's going to use the rope to catch a fish, she wraps it around her torso and hands me the other end.

"Umm.... Kenjō, what the hell are you about to do?"

"Relax."

"You're not about to dive in, are you?"

"No, this is just in case."

"Right, okay. Safety first." I don't know what to expect from her.

She clutches her spear, and in one swift motion, she stabs at the water and grabs something with her other hand, throwing it by my feet. I jump back, mouth agape. A large fish dances on the snow.

"Well done! Holy cow."

"Not a cow. A fish." She scrunches her features. I laugh. She repeats this motion another three times, then ties the fish in each knot she made with the rope.

"Supper," she says with a grin, holding up the fish above her shoulder. Strands of her hair fall over her eyes, and she whips it back.

"Impressive." I help her tie the fish with her rope, or rather hold it in place as she ties the proper knots to hold them.

No path is evident when we get to the woods. We stand staring at snowy fallen logs and brambles blocking where we need to go. To my left, the stone path keeps going but it's covered by fallen trees and overgrown shrubs. Kenjō takes out her knife from her satchel and starts wacking the forest to pave the way. I take out my pocketknife and do the same but I'm mostly using my arms. Her knife is bigger.

"I'm guessing no one uses that cemetery anymore."

"Hnn.... They do, but I don't know which way they take to get there."

"Why is it so far away?"

"Do you want to live close to a place where it is haunted by the trapped souls still in their bodies?"

I gulp. "Is that where your forager is going to be buried?"

"I don't know," she says tersely. "Lately, Alec has been feeding those bodies to the swine, to finish them off."

I grimace.

"It is kinder. If a body is eaten, it no longer suffers. It becomes one with the land."

"Oh." Sounds like a loophole. Alright, maybe Alec isn't all bad then. "What kind of beast do you think is doing that?"

She shakes her head. "A cruel one."

The howling of the wolf enters my thoughts from when I was tied up to the tree in front of her home. No, it can't be a wolf. Wolves don't play with their food like that. "I'm concerned there may be more of whatever it is."

"We've had wolves and bears but bears hardly leave the Aō because we kept hunting them."

"Oh, it could be a bear." Bears make a mess.

"Very likely. But if it *is* oumala... it will be almost impossible to find."

A magical bear that can come and go into this dimension. That's awesome... Not.

We follow the stream up a pine forest. After stepping over and ducking under at least two dozen logs, we finally reach a much clearer area, tucked away deep in the forest. Kenjō throws the fish to the ground, along with her bag.

"I think this area is hidden enough to sleep."

"I'd say so." I drop my backpack on the ground next to hers and stretch my arms.

Dusk has set and the temperature has dropped. I can see my breath when I speak. "Well, you fished, so I'll build a fire."

"I will make the clearing and lay out the blankets while you gather firewood then."

"Teamwork, I love it." I start picking up dry logs around and carrying them to the center of where we're going to sleep. Starting a fire isn't exactly my forte, I mean, it's not like I make them all the time. I can, I'm just sure Kenjō can create it faster and better. And I can feel her watching me as I rub the sticks together.

"If only I had made a bond with one of the runes to make an instant fire." Kenaz. Given that it's my mother's signature rune, I should bond with this one asap. Putting that on top of my to-do list.

"This is possible?"

"When I was eight years old, my aunt took me camping. She used to get thrilled by using her magic in front of me. "Let me show you how to make a fire," she said. And then she took out a rune, whispered its name, and the fire ignited instantly."

Kenjō laughs. "Were you surprised? You said magic is not common in your world."

"I couldn't believe it. I wanted her to do it again and again." I sigh, rubbing the sticks together. "She couldn't do any of that around my dad, he would freak."

Kenjō bends down next to me, takes the sticks, and starts to help. In a matter of seconds, a flame ignites, and I start to blow, trying to spread it. The flame catches. "We have fire," she says.

I scratch my head. "Thanks."

"We have ouma like that here." She says, "But anyone can learn yours, è? With the items?"

I take out my pouch of runes. "You mean these? I guess people can learn how to use them. These all belong to a single unit." I unravel the cord and rummage my fingers inside the pouch, pulling out a single rune. I turn it over. Kenaz. My chest tightens and I smile to myself. *Hi mom.* I glance up at Kenjō whose brows are furrowed as she stares at me. I drop the rune back in the pouch and close it.

"Here, we are born with it. Once we are bound, we lose our connection," she says.

We each take knives and start descaling and gutting the fish before washing them off in a freezing stream nearby. I watch as Kenjō skillfully skews each fish with a stick through their mouths, and then sticks them into the ground so that the fish are leaning over the fire. She glances at me as I watch her movements around the fire.

The flames dance on her warm skin, her ipani stripes

poking out of her neck and ears. "Do you know what kind of ouma you would have had if you hadn't been bound?"

She shakes her head and feels the stick on the ground to make sure it's secure.

"Is your magic very strong in your world?" she asks.

I laugh. "Let's just say, it is very rare."

She raises her brows.

"Most humans in my world don't have magic, they don't even believe in it. To be honest, I'm lucky to have an aunt who shared this knowledge with me. I'm happy I believed her."

"Can someone take your magic and use it as their own?"

"Hmm... No one can take my runes to use them. They would have to make their own because I'm bonding with mine and that's a long process. But," I recall a rune from the journal, "there is a rune that can take someone's power away from them. Not that I would ever do such a thing." I smile.

She glances at me from the fish. "So, anyone can learn? You don't need to have magic inside of you?"

What is she getting at? "Well, I do because of my lineage..."

Her eyes drop to the fire.

"You might not have your ouma, Kenjō, but you still have energy. And in my world, energy is all you need to make magic work. It might not be like mine, but it's still magic."

She digs into her bag and takes out two wooden plates and serves me a fish. My stomach opens up as the smell of cooked food tickles my senses.

"We have a plant that can do that too." She says between bites. "Take someone's power away and use it as their own."

"Oh?"

She nods. "So, there is still a way I can get ouma."

"Does it undo the binding?"

She shakes her head. "I wish it was that easy. Using this plant is looked down upon by other Ipani. And it is very illegal."

"Let me guess. You want to use it."

She doesn't respond.

"Well, I haven't known you for very long, Kenjō. But despite the illegal stuff, you seem like a nice girl. If it's illegal, it must be for a reason, right? In my family, I was taught to always abide by the rules. I was always scared into believing that if I don't, I could die, or risk someone else dying." Like my mom did because of the boy who died on her land. And now my aunt for pulling the plug on my mom. "I recently came to terms that it's all because of my family's curse."

"For you, that is true because of your curse. But here, it is how we survive," she says.

I take a bite of my fish and chew. "Just don't get yourself hurt, is all." I finish the last bits of fish and take our plates to wash them in the spring. With no city lights, the night is bright with all the stars in the sky. Purple and blue swirls flash above and collide together in an ongoing spiral dance. Down here, the world seems deadly, but from what I've seen, it's also beautiful.

When I get back, I warm my hands against the heat of the burning flames. "Are you sure you're going to be warm out here?" I ask her. She's already bundled up in her blankets, inside the half-opened tent she pitched over the branches of a tree.

"We don't have a choice."

I should have packed my tent into my backpack. It's not like I had enough time to gauge what I needed to bring. At least she brought something that's like a tent, no matter how basic it is. "Thank you for the blankets," I tell her, snuggling myself inside them. I flick a glance over to her. Her eyes are already closed. Our heads facing in the direction of the fire. It feels kind of weird sharing a tight tent.

The flickering of the flames lulls me to sleep.

I dream I'm in an icy, arid farmland. Nothing is around me for miles. The Northern lights illuminate the sky. It's so peaceful out here. I'm completely alone. And I should feel at peace. But something deep in the pit of my stomach, something is telling me to run. I can't understand why there's nothing around. I just want to enjoy the peace and Earth's light show. Aunt Liv and I always talked about coming out here together. To see the Northern lights.

A growl comes from behind and that urge to run starts to take over. It growls again, and this time I slowly spin around. But nothing's there. I don't know why I do it, but I open my mouth and scream "Nauthiz!"

Growling comes again. This time, as I slowly turn, I see it. Shadows mask the form of a large animal as it lunges at my face.

I shudder awake.

Pitch darkness surrounds me. Who put out the fire? I lean up on my elbow and tip over just enough to realize I have a little more elbow room than I did when I fell asleep.

I look toward Kenjō next to me but through the darkness, I can't make out her form. I carefully tap on the sheets next to me. "Kenjō?" My hand lands on something wet. Gross, what is that? I hold my hand to my face. Is that blood? Strands of what feels like hair stick to my fingers. I jerk back, letting out a hoarse rasp. That's blood. With hair on it!

Shit, shit, shit! I spin around, furiously, kicking the sheets off me. "Kenjō!" I quickly slip on my boots. It took her. The beast took her! I bump my head on the top of the tent and nearly fall on my face.

Cold wind whips through my hair and I squint through the night, letting my eyes adjust to the dark. The light from the stars and moon reflects off the snow. What do I do?

Frantically, I search around. If she'd just gone to the bathroom, there wouldn't be blood with hair on it where she was. I wipe my hand on my pants. I walk away from the fire pit, my heart pounding in my chest. "Kenjō!" I call again.

How did this happen?

How could I have let this happen? She was sleeping right next to me.

"Kenjō." A biting wind slaps me in the face.

She can't really be gone.

The silence of the night sends dread over the pit of my stomach. Wind flaps the side of the tent and I hold my breath to listen for her. My eyes scan the rolling hills of snow and then toward the forest. Nothing. She's really gone, isn't she? Her entrails are going to be spread around in the morning, aren't they? How could it have taken her so silently, am I really that heavy of a sleeper? Wouldn't she have screamed? Cried out for help?

Unless she didn't scream because it killed her while she was asleep. Then carried her off.

No. I can't think like that. I have to find her. She can still be alive in the woods. I try to erase the image of some beast carrying her off into the woods to rip her to shreds. I never should have convinced her to come with me.

She needed to anyway.

I get back to the half-broken tent in case she came back. I accidentally touch some more bloody hair and I hold my mouth not to vomit. Turning away, I grip onto my side pocket and feel for the runes. It's only us now.

I look from side to side. Could she have gone the way we came? Or could she have gone in the other direction?

Does she sleepwalk? No, that won't explain the blood either, idiot.

I start walking deeper into the wooded area we hadn't gone in. "Kenjō?"

No answer. I swallow my fear and keep on going. Even if just to find her body, then I'll know, and I'll have to turn back.

Something lands behind me. I pause. A low cat-like growl sends my hairs standing on end. Slowly, I turn around.

And come face to face with a very large cat. I stifle a gasp and take a step back. The cat's pupils dilate, its head prowls, and next thing I know, it lunges.

CHAPTER NINE

I INSTINCTIVELY SHIELD MY FACE WITH MY ARMS AND crouch low on the ground. The cat jumps over my body, landing on all fours behind me. With my heart in my throat, I ease back slowly, sticking my hands in front of me. "Nice kitty."

The cat has a golden coat with black spots decorating its muscular body. I've never seen a jaguar up close and personal in my life, but I'll bet money it is one. It growls, placing one paw directly in front of the other as its tail sways behind. It takes one stealthy move forward, its hind legs replacing where its front feet had been.

My eyes dart between the tent and the jaguar. Kenjō's spear. I have to find it. My eyes target the tent entrance, half-fallen.

The jaguar lets out a harsh roar and springs toward me.

I jump out of the way, toward the direction of the tent, the large cat clawing my leg as I crash land in a pile of snow.

The jaguar skids to the side and leaps in front of me, landing on the tent, blocking my ability to find any weapon, and bringing the entire tent down with it.

I fall on my back, my arms blocking my fall as I land on the ashen fire pit.

It crouches down, its head following the quick movements of my legs as I push myself back, but also keeping its large eyes on mine. It crouches lower as if it's about to make another leap but instead begins moving quickly toward me.

Ever use a string toy to get a cat to play, and it moves swiftly toward it? That, but the cat is ten times larger, and the stringy toy is me.

I back up more as it makes a right and starts circling around me. I'm a dead man.

As it maneuvers behind me, I spin on my heels, fully aware I'm sitting between the jaguar and a bag full of bombs and a knife buried in the folds of the tent.

I'm not stupid enough to think I can outrun a jaguar, but I have no other choice. Find a bomb or become kitty chow. I spring to my legs and jump for the tent.

Stabbing pain sears through my back as claws dig into my skin. I let out a hoarse scream and I let gravity pull me down. The jaguar springs up a tree. Another hoarse cry escapes my lips involuntarily. Did I scare it off with my scream?

Using my elbows, I start an army crawl to the tent.

It jumps over my body and lands in front of the tent, facing me, and blocking my potential weapons. Its tail flicks from side to side.

It's playing with me. Playing with its food. Images of the

bodies ripped to shreds from the village surface in my mind. It's trying to tire me out until it gets bored and then it will eat me.

And I'll feel the pain even after death in this world?

Hell no.

I muster up whatever courage I have left and stand up. The jaguar digs its paws into the snow, its hind legs preparing to take off. It leaps at me. I duck and block my face with my shoulder. As it strikes, I swing it around, using its momentum against it. The jaguar lands on its feet behind me.

The large cat roars, and I keep my eyes fixed on it, backing myself slowly toward the tent.

It runs at me, and I prepare to do the same thing again, except it passes me and sprints up a tree.

Odin's balls. Now it has the full advantage.

I dive inside the tent and start digging through the mess of fabric until my hands land on a bag, more blood hair, and a tiny sharp object that pricks my fingers. Ow. No time to check what that was.

A thud lands behind me, and I quickly clutch something long and sharp. The knife. Good enough. I stand, facing in the direction of the thud.

A deep-throated roar comes from behind me, and I spin around. How did it get there?

I don't see it. It's hunting me like a game of cat and mouse.

A hissing sound spins me back around.

Adrenaline surges through my veins, and I check my six.

"Where are you, stupid cat?"

The jaguar emerges from the shadows and circles around

me again, its eyes steady on me, stalking its prey. I, too, keep my eyes on its movements through the dark forest.

Squaring its face to mine, it straightens its body, preparing for the kill.

Adrenaline courses through me, and I ready the knife to strike when it lands.

It leaps into the air, and my legs still. Keeping my knife pointed straight up, my arms suddenly vibrate, and I let my knife drop.

With no time to process what's happening, a surge of power surfaces from the depths of my bones; I feel it in every follicle, every blood vessel.

My hands involuntarily shoot out just as the cat touches me, and the red silhouette of a wild ox shoots out from my body, clashing against the jaguar in a magnetic shield.

The jaguar suspends in the air before shooting backward.

The shape of the wild ox dissipates, and its rune, Uruz, sweeps the space as the jaguar lands flat against a tree, then drops to the ground with a loud thump like a sack of potatoes being dropped from a building.

My chest heaves, and I quickly stand up. I hadn't even noticed I fell. Is it dead?

Holy shit, I didn't know I could do that! Excitement and pride whoosh over me, but I bite it down. I inch toward the jaguar, who appears lifeless on the ground.

As I approach, the jaguar vibrates. I pause, readying myself to run. In a matter of seconds, its shape starts to shrink in size and then begins to transform.

What the hell is going on?

I stand, mouth agape, as the jaguar's body morphs into the shape of a woman.

Her long brown hair covers her face, her slightly pointed ears poking through. Her arms and legs cover her naked body as she lies knocked out on the ground. I gasp.

"Kenjō?" is all I can manage to say. How could this be possible? Kenjō is a jaguar? It takes me a moment to collect my thoughts and walk to the tent to dig for a blanket. When I find one, I drape it over her and hold two fingers to her neck. There's a pulse. She's breathing. I sit down across from her.

My blood drains from my face. I could have killed her. I almost did. Queasiness sets in my stomach as I stare down at the snow. I almost enacted the curse on myself, and I would have had to live with the guilt for taking her life.

I sit with my arms around my knees and my brows furrowed. Ignoring the biting cold. The sun peaks out from the horizon. It's a brand new day, and I have no idea where to go from here. Kenjō has some explaining to do.

I decide sitting here staring aimlessly isn't going to warm me up any faster. Or her... given her current wardrobe. So, I start making a fire.

I kick away debris and rocks that fell into the pit while I was being hunted and start building the logs and rubbing sticks together.

She's been a jaguar this whole time.

A were-jaguar.

Were-jaguars are real.

What the actual hell.

I mean, why not? This is a magical land with giant spiders, portals, and enchantments; of course, were-cats are real.

Sparks start flying from the friction of me rubbing the sticks, and I blow carefully.

She almost killed me.

She killed all those people. Was she bringing me out here to eat me?

The sparks die out, and my hands feel like they're about to fall off. I quirk a brow. Know what? I'm going to try something. If I bonded with Uruz, maybe I can bond with Kenaz too today. I focus on the fire pit and speak out the word Kenaz, slowly and steady. Blowing the word out with my breath. Pushing it to the world.

The image of the jaguar crashes into my mind, interrupting my concentration. Damn her.

Nothing happens. I try again.

A groan comes from Kenjō's direction as she moves under the sheets. I pause in place and stare at her. She sits up, confusion flickers on her face as she reaches toward her head, and a soft whimper comes out of her mouth. Her eyes widen as she grabs her sheets and draws them over her. She snaps her attention to me and gasps.

I slowly stand.

"What did you do?" she asks.

"Me? Are you crazy? You almost killed me."

She wraps the sheets tightly around herself and starts to back up. Her eyes fall to the broken tent, and she screams.

"Really? That's what makes you scream? I want to scream too. You scratched the shit out of my back."

She gapes at me. And then she starts to yell. In Ipani no less.

I sit, cupping my chin between my hands.

She grabs the sheet with one hand and flings her other arm at me, her eyes shooting daggers.

"I have no idea what you're saying," I yell back. "But I'd like an explanation as to why and how you almost ate me!"

Her mouth snaps shut.

"Yeah, that's right. When were you going to tell me you could turn into a freaking jaguar?"

She scoffs. "That's the best you could come up with?"

"What?"

"Me, turning into a jaguar. That's your explanation for...all this?"

"What exactly is," I move my hands the way she did, now standing up, "all this?" She stares blankly at me. "Know what?" I pull my shirt over my head. "Explain this." I turn so that she can see what I presume will be giant claw marks on my back. Which still really hurt.

She gasps. "How did that happen? I couldn't have done that. My nails are short."

"Oh, your nails are short..." my voice trails off. "You turned into a freaking jaguar. I woke up, and you were gone. I panicked and started searching for you because I thought the beast had gotten you. And let me tell you, I was so confused." I place my hand on the back of my head. "I asked myself, why would it take you and not me?"

She doesn't answer.

"Oh, and then there's the blood." I march over to the tent and pull the fallen fabric away from our sleeping area. Now that the sun is rising, I can see better. I stop at a heap of what looks to be fur mixed with blood. "What is this?" I poke it with my finger. "Is that rabbit?" I turn to her. "My fault, I thought it was pieces of *you*, but it looks like you got hungry in the middle of the night, hunted a rabbit, brought it back to the tent, and started eating it right next to me!" My chest is heaving as I'm yelling at her.

Her eyes grow puffy as tears start to well in her eyes.

"So, yeah, Kenjō. I think I'm the one who deserves an explanation."

She shakes her head, creases on her forehead deepen with confusion. "No. I-I don't know. It can't be." She grabs at her head.

"Can't be what? What are you talking about?"

Her shoulders start to shake, and she falls to her knees, her hands clutching the blankets like they're her life support. She starts rocking herself back and forth.

"Kenjō? Please don't cry." I walk over and crouch next to her. "What's going on?" She lets out a desperate wail, and her shoulders move up and down as she starts to cry uncontrollably.

"You really didn't know, did you?"

She shakes her head furiously.

"I don't understand. How could you not know you were changing?" I pinch the bridge of my nose. "All those nights you were turning, you didn't notice when you got back? The state of things, you never brought back a dead animal?"

She sobs between breaths. "I-" she takes a breath. "I never woke up to that."

"Hmm.." I guess the village is a long way from her house.

She could have left the remains at the village or somewhere in the mountain before changing back and getting home.

She dries her eyes.

"All those people. Your forager." I shake my head and wipe my face.

A low wail starts up again as she starts to cry. "I k-killed them." She stammers, crying harder.

"Oh... shit. Kenjō, hey," I inch toward her. "I'm sorry. I didn't mean to bring that up." She really doesn't remember anything. "Listen, take your time. Why don't you get dressed? And I'll build a fire, yeah?"

"I killed my villagers." She sobs.

"Not all of them?"

She shoots me a wet, dirty look.

"Sorry, I'll shut up now." I stand and reach for her bag in the tent, handing it to her so she can find her clothes. Turning my back, I start grabbing dry sticks again. Her sobs keep going as she moves around behind me. I keep my eyes glued to the fire pit. This time, successful at building a fire without trying to use Kenaz. According to the journal, Kenaz is the type of rune that requires total focus, as it represents the controlled flame. I'll never be able to bond with it without a cool head.

She's killed people. Being around her while she kills others, regardless of her knowing or not, will make me an accomplice. I still don't get it. How is it she doesn't know she can turn into a jaguar? I'm pretty sure I would know if I were a were-cat.

The flames blaze hot, and I hold my hands out. Kenjō inches closer, and I turn to her.

"Hey there." I almost say, guess you're not hungry, but I shut my mouth and get up to grab some leftover fish from last night. Her eyes follow me as I do, and for a split second, my hairs stand on end, afraid she might transform again. I sit back down in front of the fire.

"Thank you," she says.

"For what?"

"For telling me."

My brows raise and drop as I bite off a piece of fish. "You're welcome?" I don't know what to say. "How did you not know you could turn into a jaguar? I thought you were bound, no ouma."

To be honest, I'm not sure how much of this I believe. How could she not know she could shift to a large cat each night?

She shudders a breath and squeezes her eyes shut.

"Did you lie to me?"

A cold breeze wraps her hair around her face. She pushes it back. "No, I told you the truth."

"Okay, then how?"

"The Rikorō," she stammers.

I scrunch my features. "Isn't that the name of the plant you're after?"

She nods.

"Wait, the one you said was unstable?"

"Yes."

"You're going to have to give me more than one-word answers, Kenjō."

She turns her face away, averting her eyes.

"Kenjō, if you want me to trust you," I pause, "enough to keep hiking with you, I need to know who you are. I need to know the truth."

She shifts in place, then she nods. "Remember last night when I told you there was a plant that could give Ipani ouma?"

"The highly illegal one? Yeah...what about it?"

Tears start forming in her eyes again. "I didn't know if it would work," she fidgets with her hands, bending her fingers back. "I started making the potions the same way my mother told me. But... I didn't want to experiment on the captives they would bring me. So, I started taking it myself."

Oh Frigg. "You took a highly illegal plant that is unstable?"

She nods.

"Is that why you're getting nosebleeds?" She was coughing, too, if I remember correctly. "Is that stuff making you sick?"

"I think so."

"Kenjō, that can't be good. Why did the plant choose a jaguar? Is it random?"

She gets quiet, and she sniffles.

"Is it random?" I repeat.

She purses her lips together and squeezes her eyes again. Why do I feel like I'm not going to like this answer?

"In order to make the Rikorō..." she pauses. "The plant needs to be mixed with the ouma of an unbound Ipani."

My mouth drops. "I thought you said there were no more unbound Ipani, though. So how—"

"None here in Piupeki. My mother brings them from all over. As their captives."

"Wait, what? And they're okay with this?"

She shakes her head. "No, many of them get killed after. But we have a contact who can bind them."

"Alec?"

"No. He would never." Her eyes widen, and she stares me

dead in the eye. "He does not know any of this. Please, he can't."

I shrug. "Okay."

"Once the Rikorō's power takes hold, it's a ticking time-bomb. My job was to try to stabilize it. Now, it's more urgent that I find more Rikorō so that I can go back and try to..." she paces back and forth. "If I could figure out how to stabilize it..."

"Wait, you're going to keep taking more?"

"I have to mix it with the stabilizer. Just the plant itself."

"Won't it kill you?"

She swallows heavily. "It already is."

"Stop." She stares into my eyes, and I pinch the bridge of my nose. This is all too much. "You guys steal people from their homes, take their power, and...basically take it for your-selves. You guys sound like pirates."

"I have never been on a ship."

"Well, then your mom is a pirate."

Her brows arch as she stares at me. I drop my shoulders.

"How long ago did you take this Rikorō?" As in, how long has she been eating people?

She wipes the tears from her face and clears her throat. "It's been a long time already; two months."

"When did the killings start to happen?"

"Only a couple of weeks."

"That's quite a while. Does Rikorō always take long to manifest?"

She shakes her head. "It isn't stable enough to keep tabs, but theoretically, it should only take a couple of days to work.

That's why I didn't think it worked on me... unless..." Her eyes fall to the ground.

"Unless?"

"Hnn... Unless the ouma that was given to me was from a small child reaching their oumala puberty."

The blood drains from my face. From a child.

"It would make sense as to why there was a delay. The ouma wasn't mature yet."

This just keeps getting worse. "... And the child?"

She shakes her head. "I didn't ask any questions. I'm not there for that process. I only receive the vials."

I cup both hands on my face and close my eyes. I can't keep going on this journey with her. She's involved in some really bad shit. And I need to find the sword to get my portal to open, save my aunt from this curse, and not get caught up in some Ipani trafficking ring. "Is there no other way to cure you without taking the Rikorō? Something for you to take so that you don't die?"

She shakes her head. "Nothing that anyone knows about."

A sigh escapes my lips. "Talk about stupid."

"You don't understand. We do this for our kind. To save them. Imagine if we can become immune to being bound? A new generation of Ipani who could defeat the Empress. This isn't forever. It is only until we discover how to make it stable."

"While killing innocents at the same time. But the ends justify the means, right?" My mom was right; the ends never justify the means. Never.

"You couldn't understand."

"What if something like that got into the wrong hands? Could humans take it?"

"There is nothing stopping it from working on a human."

Hmm. "I don't know, Kenjō. I don't like this. I think you should get help at your hospital or wherever you go when you're sick. Not take more of it."

She chuckles dryly. "I told you already. There is no cure."

"You're going to end up killing yourself."

"Not if I experiment on a real Ipani."

Oh hell no. "Yeah, I'm out." I start to stand up. "I'm not helping you kill people. That goes against everything I believe in. And I'm not helping you kill yourself either."

"Where are you going?"

"To grab my bag."

"Why?"

"Because Kenjō," I say, grabbing onto the strap of my backpack and getting ready to turn around. "It sounds like you're in some deep operation that I cannot be a part of. I have my own mission, and being around you will jeopardize everything. The ends do not justify the means. They never do." I lift my bag from the tent, slip it on my back, and walk toward her. "You get yourself caught up in illegal stuff, like using this plant, and people end up dead. You see? Breaking the law ends with people dying, not only for my family. This is evidence that it's true for everyone. I can't stay with you. I have too much at stake. I'll find the sword on my own. Head East until I find the castle, right? Sounds easy enough." I stare out at the mountains in the East. I can't take my chances on not breaking my family's curse for someone else. The runes were right all along. I should have gone alone.

"Harold, what if I get found? You don't understand. Jaguars are not from here. They will know I am Ipani. I'll be killed on the spot."

"And so will I be if they find me next to you or if I enact my family's curse for being your accomplice. Not to mention, you might maw me in my sleep."

"What if I can control it?" She blurts.

"Good luck with that." I feel terrible leaving her like this, but she's a killer. Even if she never wanted to be. She helped in kidnappings and experiments. Or will now, whatever. I start to walk off and then turn back. "What was in that room you didn't want me to see anyway?"

She swallows. "An oumala snake. I used it to enchant the rope."

"With Rikorō."

She nods.

I shake my head and continue walking.

"Please, Harold, don't let me go into Ahan Alēla alone. Not like this... Maybe you can tie me up at night so I don't eat anyone else."

"No, Kenjō," I call out. "I don't feel comfortable tying people up."

Footsteps run after me. "You don't understand. I know I can stabilize it. I just need more."

"You sound like a junkie."

She crunches her face.

"An addict," I hiss.

She at first shakes her head. "It might nullify everything, maybe mixed with the same plant. But then my new ouma would be taken away."

"So, you'd rather keep killing people?"

She stays silent for a moment, then whispers, "I just wanted the powers they talked about."

My eyes widen. "Right. You're on your own," I say regretfully because I really don't want to do this alone. She parts her lips and then closes them, regret showing in her eyes. I turn back around and head toward the next set of woods. Hopefully, if I keep going straight, I'll find my way with the help of the runes.

I just can't get caught.

CHAPTER TEN

She calls after me, but I don't look back. As much as I want to help her, and as much as I want her on this journey with me because I have absolutely no clue how I'm going to survive this world- hell, I don't even know if I'm walking in the right direction. I can't let myself be distracted. The last thing I need is to enact the curse on myself and die here, never even getting the chance to try and face the Frost Giants.

Kenjō will only slow me down with her transforming into a jaguar. I still can't believe she didn't know. I mean, I know she's not making it up. But it's difficult to fathom.

How did she not notice waking up naked every day?

I slip away into the woods, where I can no longer hear her, and keep on walking. I think she mentioned the Eternal Mountains are after the next clearing. Or was it the one after? Flakes of snow land on my nose.

The last thing I need is for one of those creepy Arcana

soldiers to take me because they will find out what she is. All they need to do is hunt for the yeti at night and run into a jaguar. It's only a matter of time before they catch her. And I'm not going to be caught in the crossfire.

Plus, she can literally eat me. No, she can rip me up, play with my entrails, and then eat me. Oh, and apparently in this world, I'll still be feeling it even after I die. So, screw that.

Despite the cold, sweat beads down my forehead from me, keeping a fast pace.

As I immerse myself deeper into the forest, snow starts to fall heavier. My mind wanders back to Kenjō. Maybe she decided to turn back since she'd be on her own? I shake my head. None of my business. I keep walking and think of my mom and aunt, and I wonder what my dad is doing now. Probably worried sick.

The path starts to steepen as it becomes windy and narrow. I adjust my backpack and keep moving. The sky today is the complete opposite of yesterday. The clouds are overcast. It's windy and snowing.

The Rikorō is killing her. I left her to *die*. My shoes crunch on the snow as I balance myself with a silver tree.

There's nothing I could do for her anyway. She said it herself; there's no cure. I scratch at the corners of my eyes and pull away some frost attached to my lashes. I stare at the white flakes on my black gloves. It's because it's snowing. Nothing else.

Does me leaving Kenjō alone to die implicate me with the curse?

Frigg.

Something scurries off in the distance, and I pause. What

was that? It moves again next to a bush, shaking off some of the snow from its branches. I take a few steps and pause when a rabbit hops between the silver leaves. I peek closer and spot its long ears flat against its back. Careful not to scare it off, I move my hand down to my pocketknife. My stomach opens up as I realize it's been hours since I had a bit of cold fish. It nudges its head, and I pause.

It's so cute.

Oh, come on, Harold. You're in the wild, and there are no fruits or vegetables that I know of out here I can eat. I can do this. Do I want to starve?

The rabbit hops a few paces away from me, and I take one long stride, lifting my knife.

I can't. It's too cute. It'd be like killing Bambi or Thumper in this case. I lower my arm, and the rabbit suddenly turns its head. Its giant black eyes glower at me. I squint at it. The rabbit leaps into the air, and I buckle back, hitting a tree behind me. The rabbit lands by my feet. Its large black eyes squaring me straight in the face. Something tells me this isn't just a regular rabbit.

It opens its mouth to reveal double rows of piranha-like incisors and lets out a hiss. Turning to get away, I step on my own foot, twisting my ankle, and fall on my knees. I grab the tree for support, ducking behind it as the rabbit follows me. What in the Bunnicula hell is this thing?

The ground vibrates beneath my feet. The rabbit closes its mouth and looks past me. It starts to back away.

Dare I look behind me? Slowly, twisting my back, I peek over my shoulder.

Odin's balls.

A giant, completely covered in white fur— easily eight or nine feet, and four horns on its head towers over me. We lock eyes, and I almost piss myself. I clutch onto the tree bark, wishing I had brought one of Kenjō's bombs with me. Talks of an āngaraeke, or yeti, resurface in my memory when the village discussed what could be killing people.

Little did they know it was Kenjō, but I can understand why this guy was a candidate. The yeti opens its mouth and roars, snapping me back to the present. I close my eyes and mouth as spit and bad breath assault my face. I back up into the tree. When it's quiet, I open my eyes, readying myself to run.

The yeti takes two giant leaps past me and out into the narrow path. It swiftly swings its arm into the bushes at a fast pace, scooping up the rabbit. The rabbit opens up its mouth to reveal its spear teeth. In one motion, the yeti twists its head right off and chucks it over his shoulder.

My knees give out, and I crouch to the floor, still gripping the tree. I keep my eyes peeled on the yeti as it starts to sink its fangs into the rabbit's raw, furry stomach. Ripping a piece off and chewing it bit by bit. I think I'm gonna be sick.

Gripping onto the bark of the tree, I pull myself up and make a run for it. I don't even bother checking if I'm headed in the right direction. Thumping on the snow makes me look over my shoulder. The yeti, wide-eyed and alarmed by my sudden sprint, moans loudly as he advances toward me.

Ignoring the pain in my ankle, I book it even harder. A surge of power warms my chest, and Uruz comes to mind. What made me use it before?

Fear.

Protection.

The yeti swings his arm, aiming to reach me, his brows arched high above his eyes.

Going for it, I give in to my power and mouth the word, "*Uruz.*"

A wild ox emanates from my chest, casting a red aura around me in the form of the rune, Uruz. I struggle to keep my feet steady as my body wavers. It feels like the effects of the back of a magnet leaving my body as the ox smacks itself into the nine-foot giant. The yeti flies back, crashing into the bushes he had flung the rabbit bits into. The ox marches through the air, dissipating into smoke.

Resisting the urge to fist pump the air, I spin on my heel and start to run. That's twice I cast that rune, and this time it was on command. I'll celebrate later.

The yeti roars behind, me but I don't look back. I keep running. I jump over a bush, nearly falling over it because of my pained ankle. I use the trees to help me maneuver. I need to keep going. All I can think about right now is getting away.

A loud whistling sound falls from the sky and lands beside me. My heart plummets to my stomach. What are the chances they're here hunting the yeti and not here because I used magic? Another whistling sound, followed by another. Within seconds, I'm surrounded by a fog of white smoke. I spin around in search of the yeti, but it's nowhere to be found. Instead, chrome masks stare at me with their soulless eyes.

"Hi guys," I say.

They circle around me, not leaving any room for an escape. A deep red gust of smoke materializes inside the circle, and a woman emerges. She has piercing blue eyes behind a gold mask and a laurel leaf circlet on her head. Black, spidery lace decorates her cleavage and arms, with military fashion shoulder blades and a long cape-like gown, a stark contrast to the silver trees and white snow surrounding us.

Beside her, another deep blue gust of smoke emerges, but this time, it's a soldier behind a man. The smoke dissipates, and my eyes widen. It's Alec.

"Harodscot," he says, "or is it, Jutharold?" he snaps his fingers. "I can't seem to remember."

"Uh..."

The woman snaps her face to us. "Silence."

I swallow.

"Apologies, your Divinity. It appears that this is the Magician causing the magical flares the guards have been noting."

Magical flares? Does he mean my wild ox casting? So they are here because I used magic. Frigg, Kenjō warned me not to use my magic. I should have listened, not that I had a choice in either situation.

The Empress draws her eyes to me. "Show me your mark, boy." Her voice is crisp and demanding; although only visible from her mask's peepholes, her eyes have a certain fierceness that tells me she's seen a lot and is probably unforgiving to anyone who tries to talk their way out of trouble. Here comes that queasiness again.

I withdraw my arm.

She takes a step toward me. "Show me your mark. Or suffer endlessly."

Hesitantly, I lift my sleeve up and reveal the infamous "I" of the Magician.

"Search him," she snaps, turns on her heel, and leaves the soldiers to pat me down.

"Hardscot," Alec looks around him, worry lines indenting his forehead. "Where is Kenjō?"

I lift my arms up as a soldier pats my armpits. "We decided to go our separate ways." As much as I don't agree with her, I intend to keep my promise so as not to tell him. Or anyone about her transformations. My stomach dips.

What if *that* gets her killed? Then it'd be my fault.

A soldier yanks down my backpack, and I fight him to keep it on. The soldier pushes my head down with force as another soldier pulls my backpack off my shoulder. I let out a grunt.

"Don't make it harder on yourself. Best not to fight," Alec says in a lazy tone.

"But that's my stuff," I say, letting them take my bag. The journal is in there with everything I need to learn about the runes and the World Tree. "I need it back."

One of the soldiers sticks his hand down my pockets a little too forcefully.

"Hey, easy with the goods," I say to them. The one to my right side checks the pocket with the runes. Oh no... He grabs the pouch and pulls it out.

"I knew you were trouble when I saw you," he says. "Kenjō is a good girl. Now she won't be bothered by you."

Yeah, because that's exactly what it looks like. I follow my mother's runes in the soldier's hand as he takes them to the Empress.

"What do we have here?" she asks.

"Those are mine."

"Perhaps, and perhaps not anymore." She looks at the soldier. "Open it."

The soldier unravels the pouch and reveals its contents. I gulp. Please give them back, shit, shit, shit.

She reaches and grabs the pouch with a gloved hand, taking one rune out to inspect it.

"Uruz!" I scream. Like before, a wild ox bursts from my chest, the magnetism striking every soldier in the circle, including Alec. Gusts of white fog cover their bodies, for them to reappear seconds later. My knees quiver, and my eyes fall to the Empress, who stands upright and unequivocally unaffected. She closes her fingers over my mother's leather pouch, her expression hidden beneath her mask. She blinks her eyes.

In the corner of my eye, I can see Alec appearing from behind a soldier. One must have protected him from my blast.

"Seize him," the Empress says.

And just like that, soldiers are grabbing me from all directions. Alec snaps his fingers, and two more soldiers materialize with a cage. The soldier holding my backpack disappears in a gust of smoke.

"No!" I yell. "Those are mine. I need them!"

I get shoved into the metal cage and grab onto the bars just as they're shut on my face. My nose hits cold steel.

The Empress glides over to me. "I recognize alien magic when I see it. I feel the power emanating from them. What are they, and where did you come from?" she asks me.

"Those are runes. And I need them to get home." Well, I need them to get to Jotunheim and then get home, but I'll spare her the details.

"Oh, you won't be going anywhere. I'm quite interested in these...*runes.* What is your name?"

"...Harold."

"Well, Harold. Where did you emerge from? And how did you get past my guardian?"

"Your guardian? The giant spider—"

"You see, Harold, I have a strict rule in my Empire. Do you know what that is?"

"Umm... no magic?"

"Good boy. And do you know what mark you have on your wrist?"

"...The Magician's mark."

"Correct."

I sigh. "Yes, but I'm obviously not from here and—"

"Do not sass me. You will tell me how and why you are here."

"I never wanted to come here." I raise my hands up from inside the bars. "I was going to a different world and got pulled into this one instead."

"A different world?" She leans in. "Which world do you come from?" she asks slowly.

The way she looks at me makes my bones shake to their core, and I remind myself she's the Empress from the *Tarot.* "Why is that important?"

"It makes the difference on whether I should just kill you or not. Answer the question."

She seems to place importance on why I'm here and now how I got here. How did she get here? Or the Tarot, for that matter? Kenjō was adamant about this place being Ipa, before anything else. The Greek Conquest. Questions boil in my mind as the Empress becomes impatient. "Jotunheim," I lie. I fear that if I tell her earth, she'll kill me.

She straightens her back and squints. "And which other world were you trying to go to?"

"Asgard," I lie again, pushing down the queasiness rising to my throat. I hope this isn't going to lead to the enacting of my curse. But what choice do I have? It's lie or die. "To avenge my mother's death and break my family's curse," I add, hoping to sound more believable. At least that part's true.

"Avenge your mother's death?" her voice softens.

"Yes."

Alec steps up beside her. "Your Divinity, what if he's lying? He lied about not knowing why he had a mark before." The Empress looks from him to me quizzically.

"I didn't lie." I protest. "I don't lie." Except when I just did.

"My psychic scouts will determine whether he lies." She taps her index finger to the chin of her mask. I hold my breath. I forgot about them being psychic. "I don't see why people always think they need magic in order to survive, or in your case, seek vengeance, when in fact they need to trust in me and follow the rules. Despite your coming here accidentally, you learned of my laws and still broke them." She turns to leave as one of her pearly, white-masked soldiers walks straight toward me. His robes have a metal clasp at the neck of a shield and a tower at its center.

I inch back as far as I can. "No, wait. Just send me back." I clutch onto the metal bars. "You have powers, right? You can send me back?"

"And what would that tell my citizens?" She says, pausing to look over her shoulder. "That castaways will be rewarded?"

She's really on a power trip, isn't she?

The soldier stares into me; deep dark sockets replace where their eyes should be. A magnetic force pulls me in and a second later, let's me go. I feel as if my breath has been punched out of my lungs. The soldier turns to the Empress, and she lets out a sinister chuckle.

She straightens her back and faces Alec. "Take him to my tower. I'm not finished with him yet. I'll be seeing you soon, Magician." A swirl of red smoke starts at her feet, swooshing over her body in a circular motion until she's gone.

This is it. She found out I was lying, and now she's going to kill me. *In my family, lying leads to death.*

But then why not just do it here?

No, she realized something. What did the soldier tell her? It's probably about my mother's runes.

Alec walks over to the cage I'm in and squats down, giving me a disgusted look. "Looks like you're taking a trip to Rutavenye, Hardoscot." He shows me a toothy grin, and I stare at him.

This is the part where I'd plea for him to let me go, tell him I'm not a threat, blah blah. But the truth is. I need to get my mother's runes back, and if the tower is where they'll be, then that's where I need to go.

He stands, straightening his back, and turns toward the arcane army. "You heard the Empress, take him to the dungeons in her tower." He turns to one of the soldiers, "You, take me back to my station." The soldier who brought him here grabs his shoulders, and in a smog of blue smoke, they leave.

I'm left looking at three soldiers who are now closing in on the cage.

"Alright, boys, be gentle," I say.

Suddenly, I'm blinded by a bright blue light and thick blue smog.

CHAPTER ELEVEN

THE GROUND TILTS BENEATH ME, AND NAUSEA creeps up my esophagus. I can't see the soldiers any more, and I'm disoriented, plus the ringing in my ear. What the hell was that?

"Harold, move back."

"What?"

A second blast takes me by surprise, and I fling to the back of the cage. A second later, I'm being dragged out; I claw my hands into the snow and start kicking my legs. They'll never take me alive!

"Harold, stop it."

That voice. It takes my eyes a moment to adjust. A girl with long wavy brown hair is clutching onto my feet, dragging me away from the explosion. The explosions. Plural. "Kenjō?" I mutter.

"Can you stand?" She lets me go, and I climb to my feet. "We're not out of danger yet. We have to run."

I dart a look behind me. "Where are the soldiers?"

A soldier appears in a gust of white smoke, followed by another.

"They're back, hurry." She takes out another bomb and chucks it at them. A powerful blue light, followed by blue smoke, swallows their line of sight. Kenjō tugs my arm, "They can't die. Come on."

My feet start running before my brain catches up with me. The soldiers disappear in their smoke. How long before they return?

Kenjō makes a sharp right into the woods, and my eyes finally gain focus. I follow after her and into a densely wooded area. I pick my feet up high, trying to run on the snow. She followed me after I told her not to. I'm so glad she did.

Soldiers fly down all around us, blocking our path. A soldier aims his hand, and a stream of what looks like ice flies from his gloved palms. I shield myself just as Kenjō grabs me and pulls me away. The ice water bites into my back, and I let out a yell.

"Don't stop!" Kenjō yells, so I keep running, ignoring my skin burning from the ice-cold pain.

A loud popping sound makes Kenjō abruptly stop, and I slam into her back, toppling her forward. My heart sinks to my gut. They've caught us.

She holds her arm out to block me from running forward and my eyes land on a giant beast covered in fur. The Yeti.

My mouth gapes open. "Don't worry Kenjō, I got this one."

"What? No, Harold!"

"I can summon the ox again," I pant, out of breath.

She throws herself in front of the yeti. "Don't!"

"What are you doing?" My teeth chatter. "That thing is about to eat us!"

"No, he isn't." She turns around and holds out her palm. Backing up, the yeti lowers his head to stare at it.

More of the arcane army zooms down from the sky. "Kenjō, we don't have time for this-"

The yeti presses his enormous palm to hers, and she grabs me from behind. A loud popping sound makes me jump, and a second later, my surroundings are gray.

She lets go of me, and I slowly back away from the yeti. Holding her hand to her heart, she closes her eyes and bows her head. The yeti does the same, then turns to eye me suspiciously.

It feels like I'm in a black and white movie. "What just happened?" I ask, keeping my eyes on the yeti.

"We are in the Aō."

I blink a few times. She's mentioned the Aō before. "The dimensional world? How?"

"Shh," she holds her finger up to her mouth and points. Between the trees, two Arcana soldiers advance, with Alec following behind them.

"Clear," Alec shouts. "The Yeti grabbed Harodscot. He'll be shredded to bits, surely. Let's go." One of the soldiers grabs Alec's shoulders, and they each disappear in gusts of white smoke.

"Yetis are oumala," Kenjō says. "He has the ability to bring us in and out of it."

I gape out to where Alec had just been. "They couldn't see us." I take a few painful steps forward. "How?"

"Not while we're in the Aō. But we'll wait here a bit longer in case they come scouting the area for the yeti."

I swallow and turn to face her. She saved me. "Kenjō..." I reach for my back and grab at the ice. Blood drains from my face. My backpack is gone, and I'm covered in ice.

"We need to get you to warmth. Just try to hold on a bit." She stares at me. Strands of hair are pressed against her flawless skin as the wind passes through. She starts to unbutton her coat. "Take off your coat and take mine."

"No way. You need yours. I'm fine." I shake my knees, trying to keep warm. "Thank you for saving me back there."

She already has her coat off as she approaches me and grabs onto my back, pulling down hard on my jacket. "Ah!"

"Hold still."

Cold wind passes through my cold, wet body until she drapes her coat over me. I take it graciously and put it on. She takes my coat in her hands and folds it.

"Aren't you going to be cold?" Although, her long sleeve shirt is made of leather, lined with wool underneath. She's been a lot warmer than I have. Plus, she can turn into a jaguar and have her thick coat keep her warm.

"My blood runs warm anyway," she says. "We'll dry your coat by a fire, and I could wear it," she grins.

I give her a half smile. I'm still freezing, but this is already better. She can keep my coat then. "Thanks for that, and for saving me...But we still can't go on together. I'm sorry." I turn to leave.

"Harold, wait. You can't leave the yeti's bubble, or they'll see you. Besides that, you'll freeze to death out here. Let me help you."

I pause and look above my head. "How far does this bubble go?"

"As long as we're near the yeti, we're fine. When we leave, we'll walk out toward the sun. I will make a fire to get you warm."

I stare at the yeti and rub my hands together. "I thought he wanted to eat me earlier."

"Yetis are docile and becoming extinct for their horns."

"And being blamed for shredding humans to pieces, apparently." My voice sounded drier than I intended. Kenjō's shoulders drop, and her eyes get red again.

"I'm sorry—I didn't mean that."

She tucks her hair behind one subtly pointed ear and stands upright. "I know you will never understand my and my mother's role in all this."

I look down and scratch the back of my head.

"But I thought about what you said, and—" she sighs. "I think with the right mixture, I can stabilize the Rikorō to try to extract the ouma out of me."

I roll my eyes. "Using the same illegal plant?"

"Yes. Many poisons can be used for their alternate uses. It'll take a lot of experimentation, but I think I can do it safely, without harming anyone else."

I glance up and stare into her dark brown eyes. She stares right back at me. "So, no more killing?" Should I believe her?

"I never wanted to hurt anybody," her voice trembles. "That's why I experimented on myself."

I nod. I suppose that's true. "Well, you did just save my skin. And, if you're not going to kill anymore, I guess we can hike together." I'm ignoring the fact that she's still going to be using an illegal plant, but things have been weird since I left my bedroom. What's one illegal plant?

I turn to the yeti, and he stares at me back. I take a few steps forward. "Sorry about earlier," I say. "I thought you were going to bite my head off like you did that rabbit. By the way," I look at Kenjō. "Your rabbits are vicious."

My teeth chatter.

She scrunches her features. "We should get out of here." She faces the yeti, who lets out a moan. "The yeti can lead us to safety."

I glance in the direction of the woods, where the soldiers were landing. It's been quiet. Maybe they gave up on looking for me. A sinking feeling reaches my gut, and I grab onto my hair. Oh no. My mother's runes. This is all wrong. Nothing has gone right for me since the moment I stepped through the portal. I'm never going to get to Jotunheim now. What a stupid plan that was! Face off Frost Giants? Now I'm stuck in some Tarot world, and I'm never going to make it. My aunt is going to die because of me. My breathing quickens, and I clutch my chest.

Get a hold of yourself. I need to get them back. That's all. I *will* get them back.

"Harold? What's wrong?"

"The Empress took my mother's runes. I can't go, Kenjō. I'm sorry. Thank you for coming after me and helping me, but... I was prepared to go to the Tower."

"That's a bad idea, Harold. Nothing good can come from that."

"You don't understand, even if the sword is able to open a portal, I can't leave here without them. They were my mother's, and I just started bonding with them. They're a part of me now. I can feel it." All those stories my mother told me as a child are resurfacing in my mind. Each time I used Uruz, I felt them in my bones. This is who I am.

"I understand, but this is magic we're talking about. They are illegal, è? She isn't ever going to give them back to you. She'll have them hidden away where you won't be able to find them. She'll try to harness their power, or worse. She'll turn you into one of her soldiers."

I hadn't thought of that last part. "Can she do that? I'm not Ipani."

"It won't matter. She has done it to humans who have betrayed her."

My heart thuds loudly in my ears.

The yeti makes a noise and turns to leave. She starts to follow. "I would stay far away from Rutavenye if I were you."

"How else am I going to get them back?" I say, following them closely to stay within his Aō bubble. My teeth chatter as I walk with my arms wrapped around me. I have to get them back. I won't believe that I lost them forever.

She gives me an apologetic look. "For now, we focus on not freezing. Then, we will come up with a plan that does not involve going to the Tower, è? How is your foot?" She nudges her nose down at my foot, noticing me limping.

"My ankle?" I lift it to the side. "Pretty numb, but I'm sure it'll hurt like hell later."

Worry lines crease her forehead.

"I'm okay. I just need to rest." I definitely can't stay out here.

We follow the yeti up the mountain until we reach a gray

gorge covered in snow. The walk was long and strenuous, and I can no longer feel my toes. My nose feels like it's about to fall off. I glance at Kenjō, and even her face has turned a bit mauve from the cold.

The yeti makes a grunting sound and points toward an enclosed caved area, where a fire blazes in its center. All along the stonewalls of the grotto are deep caverns stacked on top of one another. Yetis stare at us from their openings. Woah. I follow without asking any questions. I'm one frozen Han Solo away from being carved out of ice.

I sit at the fire and let the heat thaw me out. I wish I still had my backpack. Without the journal, I'm lost on learning the rest of the meanings of the runes and anything about my family's curse. But without an extra change of clothes, I might freeze to death.

Kenjō stretches out my frozen coat by the fire. Her hands are shaking, and I stand up to help her sit. She may not have been blasted with ice, but it's still freezing for her too.

Yetis circle around us and stare like we're animals in a zoo. The yeti we followed here approaches us, and I swallow, my eyes moving up to about ten feet of fur. A groan escapes his mouth as he extends his arm out to us.

My brows furrow, and I glance at Kenjō, who's starting to stand. "Come," she says.

"How can you tell what they're saying?" I stand, reluctant to leave the warmth of the firepit.

"He decided to bond with me to communicate, but only through images and emotions."

"Oh." So far, we've been able to trust him. But without knowing anything about them, I'm still hesitant to get too close. What if the rest of them disagree with the yeti who brought us here?

We let him lead us through a mountain tunnel to a cavern of stone. Torches, emanating a red light, illuminate the path and continues into a circular cavern. Inside, hot fumes emanate from a body of water with hot springs. My fingers and knees already start to feel less chattery. The yeti turns to us and points to the water.

Kenjō bows her head and gives him thanks. The yeti looks at me next, so I mimic her actions, hoping I'm doing it right. Hey, a hot jacuzzi inside a cave? This is exactly what the doctor ordered.

Kenjō walks toward the hot water and starts taking off her shoes. I glance back at the yeti, who's already walking to the tunnel passageway, leaving us alone. I unbutton Kenjō's coat she so graciously lent me and place it on a stone boulder against the cavern wall. I take everything off except my boxers and turn to step inside the hot spring.

When I look up, Kenjō is completely undressed. Her hair covers her breasts as she steps into the water. Delicate stripes start from the edges of her back muscle and cross to meet at her center, the sharp tips of her strips barely touching. I've never seen anything like her before in my life. I quickly avert my eyes.

Ipani girls are *not* shy. Noted.

Think of something else. Anything else. I step one foot into the hot water, allowing the fumes to submerge me in a cocoon of warmth.

Kenjō giggles, and I flick my eyes to her. She sinks her body up to her shoulders, the bubbles and fumes masking the rest of her. Her hair is now tied up in a high bun, with a few strands touching the nape of her neck. Her subtle pointed ears reflect off the dim red flames from the torches.

"What's so funny?" I smirk.

"Why are you coming in with your clothes on?"

"I'm not... I'm just leaving these on."

She stares at me, her eyes going from my pecs to my waistline; she clears her throat and looks away. "That makes no sense. You should let them dry, or you will get sick."

I try to hide the smile slipping onto my face as I step deeper into the water, submerging myself up to my chest, then reach down and remove my shorts. I squeeze the water out of them at the edge of the spring and lay it out to dry. "There. Hopefully, it dries a bit when we get out."

Kenjō shakes her head and smiles.

A few beats of silence pass between us, and I awkwardly look at the stonework around us, digging in my mind for conversation to ease the silence. "So," I say. "Yetis. They're... smart and interesting."

"Yes, it is a shame they have been chased into hiding. They are known to be generous without wanting a trade in return. Some say they are drawn to people with honor. People have taken advantage of that in the past, so they are in danger of extinction."

"That's awful. We have that problem where I come from too. Not with yetis but of the hunting of other animals." I let my body relax into the water and let my arms drift.

"Are you feeling better?"

"My teeth have stopped chattering, so yes. You?"

"Yes. We were lucky to run into the yeti...How is your ankle? These are healing waters, you know."

My eyes widen. Come to think of it, I haven't felt the pain in my back or my ankle since I stepped in. I had completely forgotten about it. I rotate my ankle under the water. "This is amazing," I say.

She beams at me. "I have been thinking, after this, I should leave you."

"What? Why? I said we could hike together. You don't want to now?" The fumes cover the space between us, but it does nothing to stop my mind from wandering below the water. Focus Harold.

"You know why," she says. "I have to keep going, far from people. In case I might...you know."

"Then, I'll come with you."

Her eyes light up momentarily, and then she shakes her head. "No, I don't want to put you in danger."

Now having her here by my side, especially after she saved me, I don't want her to go. "Kenjō, I'm sorry about what I said. You're not a bad person. I mean, you came back for me. Thank you."

"I sense you are a caring person, Harold," she says softly. "You would have done the same for me."

"How did you know I was in trouble?"

"I-" She gives a modest shrug. "Honestly, I could smell your scent and decided to follow you."

I resist the urge to laugh because... that doesn't sound creepy at all. "Maybe it's a jaguar thing?"

"I think so." Her voice goes somber.

"Have you had any more nosebleeds?"

Her eyes meet the water, and she nods quietly.

A sigh escapes my lips. "I don't want you to go. If nothing

else, we're safer together. We can tie you up at night like you suggested." Not to mention if we separate, she could die from the Rikorō, and I would never know. I couldn't live with myself, not knowing if I left her to die on her own. At least this way, I can keep an eye on her. I need my runes back. If only I could bond with a healing rune, maybe it could draw out the poison from her bloodstream. My throat dries. If only that had been enough for my aunt to do to break the curse. I shake those thoughts away. I don't want to think about that right now.

"If I become too dangerous, we need to separate."

"You mentioned that maybe you could learn to control it?"

She shrugs. "If we weren't bound, we would need to learn to control our ouma, so I was thinking, why would this be different?"

"It's settled then. We'll hike together."

She doesn't respond but gets up to walk out of the springs, giving me a full view of her beautiful curves. I bite my lip hard and look down.

"I'm going to sit by the fire," she says. "The fumes here are getting to my head. Are you coming?"

I'm definitely not about to stand right now. I turn around to face the wall behind us. "I'll be there soon."

CHAPTER TWELVE

THE FIRE PIT HAS A RED DOME AROUND IT, emanating a glorious heat. This is one magic I wish we had from the beginning of our trip. From what Kenjō explained, they added a type of powder to the flames, which created this amazing heat dome. Even our clothes are fully dry, which by the way we are both wearing. Fully.

The yeti drops a dead antelope by our feet and lets out a loud groan. I bring my feet in. That's revolting. Kenjō laughs and thanks him. She crosses her heart with her fist and closes her eyes, bowing her head. The yeti does the same. She glances at me over her shoulder, "I'll help them skin and clean this to cook on the fire, then we can go after we fuel up."

Oh, thank the gods.

Who knew yetis were so hospitable?

While Kenjō helps prepare our food, I take to sharpening our knives. My mind wanders to my mother's runes, and the queasiness enters the pit of my stomach. This time, not because of something illegal I'm doing, but because I lost the only piece of her I had. I'm angry that my plan's been derailed, but I'm angrier that I lost her magic. I hadn't realized it until now, but this whole time it was like my mother was with me, in the form of those runes. Or that they're actually alive with a piece of her in them.

Two hours later, Kenjō serves us antelope steak and sits down next to me. Yetis come up, take bits of their portion of food, and walk away. They don't seem like the "let's all sit for a meal" type of group, but it's oddly different from how the yeti ate the rabbit in the woods. Maybe they have table manners.

I stare at my half-eaten piece of antelope and rest my head on my hand.

"You need to finish eating that, Harold."

"Hm? Oh, I'm not really hungry."

"You have to. They will take offense if you don't."

I quirk a brow and glance at the yeti staring at my food. "Oh. Sorry." I take another bite and start to chew. "Mmmm."

The yeti groans.

"What do we call him? Does he have a name?"

"Nothing we can pronounce, but... we can think of one for him."

The yeti groans again, eyeing us suspiciously. Can he understand us at all? I guess he can feel Kenjō's energy. Three other yetis gather around the fire and take a seat.

"Batman," I say.

Kenjō's brows knit together. "Bat man? He isn't a bat, Harold. He's a yeti. And that is like calling a dog a cat or something. I don't like it."

I stifle a laugh. Fair enough. I stare at the flames, trying to think of a good name for a yeti, but my mind is somewhere else. I stand and start pacing around the fire. My mother's runes are gone, and so is my journal.

"Harold?"

"I need to get my mother's runes back." The yetis watch my movements as I pace back and forth. "Why couldn't the soldiers and Alec see us inside of the yeti's Aō dome? They have magic. Why couldn't they find us?"

"Because they use the Empress's magic. The Empress doesn't have the ability to enter the Aō, and she thinks ouma is evil, so she does not trust oumala animals, not that any of them would bond with her. And so, her soldiers cannot cross either."

"But she puppeteers their magic for her own gain?"

Kenjō shrugs. "Once ouma has been bound, they lose connection to the Aō, so they lose connection to their spiritual source that fuels their ouma. Being able to enter and leave cannot be orchestrated externally, like with a potion."

I rub my chin. "I wonder if a soldier was ever taken into the Aō, if they would regain their consciousness and free will."

"You would have to take one to find out, but good luck. No one can capture a soldier; they just disappear before you get near them."

Alright, so what happened next? They saw the yeti and saw me disappear with him. I don't think they even noticed Kenjō. She was so quick with her bombs, wasn't she? I suppress a smirk. "Okay. The guards think the yeti grabbed me and ate me."

The yeti groans.

"No offense." I wince at him. "I can use that to my advantage. They think I'm dead. And if they think I'm dead, there's no reason for Demitri to send his scouts to spy on me. But he will want to make sure you're okay."

"Any chance you could ask Demitri to get my mom's runes back for me?"

"He won't do it. He still has to follow her laws."

"Yeah, I didn't think so." I keep pacing back and forth. What would the runes tell me if I could ask them right now? What would my aunt tell me to do? She'd tell me to think of the stories from the Hávamál.

"I remember a story about when Thor lost his hammer."

"Who?" Kenjō eyes me tentatively. The yeti yawns.

"It's from mythology in my land. Thor was a god who wielded a hammer so strong that few could carry it. It was powerful enough to get him through anything, stop anyone. And one day, he lost it."

"Did he ever get it back?"

"In the story, he finds out that Thrym, a frost giant, stole his hammer. Thor went to ask him what he wanted in exchange for his hammer back, and Thrym wanted to marry Freya. Thor's adoptive sister."

"That is disgusting. This does not happen in Ipa-"

"This is an old legend. Let me finish. Freya said no. But Heimdall-"

"Who is that?"

"At the moment, his advisor." I smack my face but laugh, "and guardian of the rainbow bridge. He advised Thor to lie and tell Thrym he can marry Freya but to then disguise himself as her at the wedding."

Kenjō's eyes widen, and she taps her lip.

"Thor's adoptive brother Loki, a real mischievous guy,

you'd hate him, went as Thor's bridesmaid just in case things went bad. When Thrym tried to kiss Thor, he recoiled. But the hammer at that point was close enough to him and returned to him."

"What happened to Thrym when Thor got his hammer?"

"Oh... Thor crushed the skulls of all the Frost Giants at the wedding."

She gasps. "Okay, and what does this have to do with you finding your runes from the Empress, è? Are you going to disguise yourself as a guard or something and go to the Tower?" Her eyes widen. "Harold..."

My mouth splits open. "Wish I had thought of that, but I'm not clever enough. No. I'd have no idea how to get the robes for that, let alone disappear like a real Arcana soldier." Not that I'd have the guts to do it either... "First, I'll get the magical portal opening sword. Then I can use the fact they think I'm dead to my advantage and sneak around to get my mother's runes."

"Yes, and I will get my plant as well. But where are you going to sneak to? You can't make it to the Tower."

"I'm going to do like Thor and march into Alec's office—or quarters, and ask him what he wants in exchange for his help in getting my mother's runes back."

Kenjō's mouth gapes. "Are you insane? He'll trap you instantly, at first sight. He'll get you killed."

"I can be persuasive when I need to be."

"This is a death trap, Harold."

"Just like your plan is a death trap?"

She snaps her mouth shut and folds her arms.

"Exactly. Look, without the runes, my time here is

extended, which means I have to do whatever it takes to get to Jotunheim to find a way to break my family's curse. Unless you know of another way I can go home? You said before you heard of others who have traveled here before."

She shakes her head. "Old legends, but I'm afraid I do not."

"Where are Alec's quarters anyway?"

"*Ruta Helāni,* the *Prefect's Tower* is on the way to Pea Memoé, but on the coast. We have to be careful they don't spot us, and we might need to leave the yeti behind before we reach there. It isn't fair to him to come with us and hide in the Aō the entire time. If he gets bored and pops out of it..."

"It works out then. First, I get the sword and your plant. Then on the way back, I make a detour to Alec's Tower. This has to be my plan. I need my mom's runes."

"In that case, maybe I can help."

"How?"

"I can turn into a jaguar. If I am successful in learning to control it, I can be your backup. In case things go bad. Like Loki." She grins.

I don't know why, but her mentioning my mythology back at me sends butterflies in my stomach. A smirk creeps on my face, but I bite it down. "That can be dangerous. They could kill you."

"Harold, I'm already...sick."

"Don't say that. You're going to figure out a way to cure yourself."

"We don't know if it will work."

"You're a great potion maker. You invented a smoke-screen bomb. I believe in you. You have to try."

She nods. "Either way, you need backup. And they think

the yeti was the one doing the killings now. Alec won't be expecting a jaguar, especially if I can learn how to go into the Aō... but that I will have to practice."

The flames dance on her face, the red ambiance giving her an amber glow. I don't like this. If I leave her alone, I'm leaving her to die. If I go with her to the plant, I'm an accomplice in harboring an illegal plant. And bringing her with me endangers her life. No matter which way I spin this, my curse can become enacted. My aunt wasn't kidding when she told me anything can lead to death for our family. At the same time, she's going to use the plant for good this time. "Are you sure about this? It's going to be dangerous."

Her eyes grow sad. "We both have lost our mothers and have curses on us, in one way or another. If I die from the Rikorō, at least let something good from it."

An anvil lands in my gut as she struggles to keep the tears from her eyes. "We better get to training you then." However we're going to manage training someone how to shift into a jaguar and disappear into another dimension is beyond me.

"I have the perfect name for him," I say, turning to the yeti, looking at his feet, seemingly uninterested in our conversation.

"È? What name?"

A grin spreads on my face. "Alfred."

"I like it."

CHAPTER THIRTEEN

"Are you sure Alfred isn't going to flip out once you turn into a large cat with claws?" Although his claws are enormous so I'm not sure if he'd be scared or not.

Kenjō throws the remaining scraps of bones at the fire as we finish off our breakfast and get ready to leave the grotto. "I showed him my memories, and he seems to understand."

"Are we staying in the Aō the entire time?" I zip up my now warm coat up to my neck and slip my gloves on.

"As long as Alfred lets us. But we mustn't take him close to the Prefect's Tower. Alec will have oumala animals protecting the area from within the Aō. And they are looking for yetis."

"Right, they think the yetis are doing the killings." I shudder to think what other oumala animals are lurking in the dimensional world... watching us, waiting to pop out at us at any minute.

Alfred groans.

Once again, we go into the frozen hell that is Piupeki, aka

swords. The yeti grotto disappears out of view as we leave the gorge. Unfortunately, being inside the Aō doesn't make it any less cold. First, get her plant as it is from the forest before the temple, Naó, then grab the sword, and onto the Prefect's Tower, where I will use the sword to get Alec to help me get my runes back. A sense of queasiness surfaces in my gut. I hope this plan works.

"Any clue as to how far away we are from the forest?" I ask.

"About a day's journey."

"Are there any villages nearby?"

"Yes, why do you ask?"

"Oh, just wanting to make sure we stay clear of them, that's all."

She fixes her jaw and stares straight ahead. Not sure if she took that as a direct comment toward her or not.

We make our way back to the path less traveled. Despite us traveling through Alfred's Aō bubble, I still have a sense of dread in the pit of my stomach. It's not that I'm worried about Kenjō eating me, although the thought is lingering in my mind. What if she leaves in the middle of the night, gets lost, or makes her way to a nearby village and tears someone to shreds?

"Have you tried to shift at will yet?" I ask.

"No, after you left, I-" She stammers. "I needed some time to try and remember. I don't understand why I can't remember... doing those things."

"I kept thinking about that too. How is it that you got home naked and didn't notice when you woke up?"

Her cheeks turn a dark shade of maroon.

"Unless you sleep in the nude, then I guess it wouldn't have mattered." When she doesn't respond, I glance at her. Right when I thought her cheeks couldn't get any redder, she looks away to hide her blushing cheeks. Of course, she does. Why wouldn't she?

"I do not."

"It's okay if you do. I'm just trying to make sense of it." I don't know why she's being shy now all of a sudden. She wasn't shy back at the hot spring. Maybe it's because she knows I'm thinking about her...

"What would happen if the sirens go off at night or there's a fire to my tree, and I have to leave fast, è? It is always cold in Piupeki."

"Okay, I get it."

"I am always wrapped up when I sleep."

"Sure thing. Still doesn't explain how you wouldn't have noticed."

"I know," she snaps. "I am trying to remember."

I turn back to Alfred. "How bout you? Do you remember the first time you ever went into the Aō?"

He lets out a quizzical moan. At least, I think it's quizzical.

"Did it just happen, and you freaked out?" or maybe he had parents there to show him what to do.

He grunts.

I turn around to face the yeti completely, walking backward. "Is that so? How'd that make you feel?"

Kenjō laughs. "Stop tormenting him."

"Nah, I think he can understand more than we think." I spin back around.

"Oh, I know he can," she says. "He can see emotions, so he knows you're not a threat."

I crane my neck to Alfred, who's looking at the ground as we walk. "Alright, how about you try to shift forms?" I ask her.

"Into a jaguar, right now?"

"Yeah, that was the plan, right? For you to be stealthy enough to back me up later?"

She glances at me, then faces forward.

No? Is she not going to try? Okay, maybe it's too soon. She starts to stretch her arms. Oh, we have movement!

A cold breeze passes through my hair, and the trudging of our boots on the snow is the only thing I hear.

Any minute now.

I turn back to Alfred and shrug. He twists his furry features and lets out a soft huff from his nose. Is she doing anything? I walk a little faster so that I can see her face. Her forehead is wrinkled, and her lips are puckered as she concentrates hard on the ground in front of her. I burst out laughing.

"È? Why are you laughing?"

"I'm sorry, I can't help it. What are you doing?"

"Trying to shift."

"You look constipated."

She scowls at me. "I am trying to focus."

"Okay, okay. I'll be quiet. Please, try again."

She shoots me a dirty look and goes back to staring straight ahead of her. She pulls her satchel over her shoulder and swings it back at me. It hits my chest with an unexpected thud as I grab onto it.

"What are you giving me this for?"

She starts to run at a full sprint, and I startle. Alfred jumps forward, but I hold his arm back. He pauses and looks back at me. "I think she's going for a running start," I say, shouldering her bag. He grunts and stares out to where she ran. "Come on, might as well follow."

The ground lifts at another steep incline as we head toward the mountain. My thigh muscles ache as if I've been hiking for almost a week. Oh wait, that's exactly what I've been doing.

Kenjō stops at a tree up ahead, turns around, and sprints back, lifting her knees up high as her hands move rapidly back and forth. I do not envy her right now.

She pushes past me at full speed, nearly crashing into Alfred. I reach into her satchel and hand her her canteen as she pants in place. She takes it from me and takes a swig.

"I'm guessing you wanted to give yourself a running start into jaguar mode?"

She hovers over her knees, still out of breath, and nods.

"It didn't work."

Her eyes shoot up at me, and she grimaces. "You are not helping."

"I'm sorry," I say between laughs. "I know. I wish my aunt was here. She'd know what to do."

"And what would your aunt do, hn? She does not know Ipa anymore than you do."

What would she say to Kenjō if she were here? Probably what she always tells me. To trust myself. Listen to my intuition.

I take off her satchel and place it on the ground. "So, shortly after my mom fell and Aunt Liv came to live with us, I was having trouble coping at school."

"What is school?"

"Oh, it's where children go to learn. Do you have something like that here?"

She shakes her head. This might be tricky to explain. "Well, in school, we get graded for our assignments and tests…"

"I know tests."

"Right, so my grades not only took a hit, but I had trouble keeping friends." Kenjō squints her brows, but I keep going. "One time, my dad invited my best friend over to play catch because he thought it would cheer me up. I told my friend to go home. When he asked me what was wrong, I told him my mom was in a coma. He said, "That happened three months ago. Get over it."

"That's when I hit him. Clocked him right in the jaw."

Kenjō's eyes widen, and she laughs.

"My aunt came running and pulled me away, but I was fuming. Get over it? I'd give him something to get over. My dad drove my friend home, but my aunt stayed with me and calmed me down." Kenjō places her hand on my arm. I take a deep breath.

"She was the only person with the gift of calming me," I say. "Now that I think of it, those little meditations she used to guide me with got me through life. I bet I could apply that here." *Find your mother in your heart. You know it's always there. Sense it. Feel it.* My chest tightens.

"You were lucky to have your aunt with you. Your friend was just a little kid, è? And you had so much anger. But how could that help me here?"

"Okay," I say. "Let's stop for a minute." I rub my hands together, trying to stay warm.

"È?"

"Just relax your shoulders."

"Why?"

"Trust me."

She arches a brow. "Hnn."

"What? Oh, come on, you trust me." I smirk.

She gives me a scrutinizing glare, then straightens her back and closes her eyes.

"Good. Take a few deep breaths and clear your mind. Think of the darkness in your mind, where it's most quiet." Giving her a few seconds to do that, I shift focus to the yeti. He stares at her, shifting his gaze between me to her. "Are you calm?" I ask her.

She scoffs. "Mhmm."

"Now, listen to my words. Inside that darkness is you. All of you is filled with everything you've ever experienced and everything you've ever learned. This new magic you have—ouma, is now a part of you. At night, it takes hold of you, but you know it's always there. Sense it. Feel it. You can reach it again and shift at will."

The lines in her features tense as she focuses. The corner of her lip twitches, and she bursts out laughing.

I sigh. "Really? That was my best Aunt Liv impersonation too."

"You sounded so serious."

"I'm trying to help you, Kenjō."

"I'm sorry." She grabs her stomach, still laughing. After a few moments, she straightens her face. "I'm sorry, I can't. Maybe I can only shift at night because I'm nocturnal."

"Yeah, maybe. It's okay. It's best if you don't help me. Stay safe instead."

"No, I want to help. I can do something else. I still have a few bombs left."

Alfred takes a step forward, holding out his hand. She looks at it, and then he pokes her shoulder.

I scrunch up my features, and we exchange confused glances. A second later, she disappears with a loud pop.

I gasp and gape at Alfred. "What happened?" I look around us. "Kenjō? Where'd you go?"

She pops back and gasps.

"Woah, what happened?"

"I went into the Aō."

"Just by him touching you? By yourself?"

"Without him, yes."

We both stare at him.

"That felt..." Her legs start to shake, and she falls to the ground.

"Woah, what's happening?"

Her arms start to shake next, and then her entire body. Her hands and feet shrink, her face narrows, her eyes slant. Her hair becomes one with her body as she starts to shift before my eyes.

Her head shakes furiously, and she steps away from her clothes. She looks down at her feet and does a circle, sniffing the air.

"Kenjō?"

She pauses, her head snapping in my direction.

"Kenjō... easy now. You just shifted."

She licks her lips and digs her paws into the snow.

"Kenjō, it's me, Harold." I do my hardest to hold my ground despite my impulse to run kicking in. "Remember who you are."

Alfred backs up, eyeing her.

She lunges at me, but before I can run, she pins me down. I

bring my feet up and flip her over my head. She catches her footing, spins around, and stares at me.

Not this again. "Kenjō, come on, it's me."

She jumps at me, but Alfred intercepts. He sticks his claws out and misses by an inch.

"Careful," I yell, "you'll hurt her!"

Alfred yells at Kenjō as she switches her focus between the both of us.

"Kenjō," I crouch low to the ground. "You're still in there. Try to remember."

A hissing roar sends shivers through my bones.

I start to back up, ready to fling her over my head if she leaps at me again. Instead, she leaps to a tree next to us. I straighten myself up and back up closer to Alfred, who hasn't moved, his eyes now on the tree. I wish I had my mom's runes. I try summoning Uruz. If only I could feel it. If I could somehow summon its energy and bring out the wild ox.

Kenjō leaps down.

And I feel nothing. No power. Just immobilizing fear. A cracked yell escapes my lungs as I bring my arms up to block her. Searing pain shoots up my arm as she claws at my forearm on her way down. I backpedal right as Alfred hits her with a powerful blow to her backside, making her skid off me and turn her attention to him.

This is useless. She does not remember who she is, and I don't want to hurt her. There's got to be a way for her to remember who she is when she shifts.

Kenjō slowly walks around Alfred, spinning him around, but he doesn't run. What's he going to do? With one loud roar, she leaps at his face. Alfred lifts his arm and smacks her face so hard she flings into the air. I gasp.

Kenjō flips through the air and lands on her feet.

"Kenjō?" Afraid to get close to her, I share a look with Alfred and inch toward him instead.

Her head bobs, and she lies down.

"I think you hit her too hard," I tell him. "She looks like she got a concussion."

He groans at me.

Her body starts to tremor, and I gape at her. Her hair lengthens as her arms and legs become human-like. Her Jaguar spots, lengthening to show the stripes of her Ipnai skin. And she's naked.

She takes in a long gasp of air.

"Kenjō? Are you alright?" I quickly find her clothes on the far side where we had been when she turned. I grab them and toss them by her side, turning around to give her some privacy. Alfred plops down on the ground.

She fumbles around for a few minutes. "It's alright, Harold. You can turn around."

"Are you hurt?" I ask her. "It looked like he hit you pretty hard."

"My head hurts, but I'm okay." Her eyes widen, and she gasps. "Harold, your arm! I'm sorry!"

Blood stains my shredded jacket from where she struck me with her claws. She reaches into her satchel and pulls out a rag, then walks over and grabs my arm, wrapping it with her cloth.

I suck in a hiss as it touches my wound. "Thanks... It's just a scratch. I'll be fine."

"I should go back. I'm a hazard to you, Harold." Her eyes

are glued to her handiwork on my arm, and creases wrinkle her forehead as she deepens her frown.

"No, I told you I'd help. I meant it. You need help, Kenjō. Not someone who will abandon you."

Her lips curl into a weak smile as she lets my arm go.

"Do you remember being a jaguar?"

Her brows furrow as she looks off to the side. "No... I feel like... I took a nap and don't remember my dream. It's so strange because I got up out of breath. Like I had been running all day."

"Well, you definitely ran. And leaped. And lunged at my face."

"Sorry."

"And at Alfred's face." I glance at Alfred, who groans. "It's okay. It's progress. You went into the Aō, and you shifted."

"Because of his help," she glances at Alfred, who has a bored look on his face, apparently no longer interested in Kenjō as she's not a threat anymore. For the time being.

"But it's a step closer. How was he able to do that to you, anyway? Do you know?"

She shakes her head. "We don't know too much about yetis. They stay away from us for good reason. Somehow, he was able to pass his ouma to me, and my body remembered."

I rub my chin. "If it wasn't that he did it to you, but that your body remembered, that's a good thing. Maybe the more you practice, you'll be able to shift on your own."

"Maybe I'll try again later. I've had enough of blacking out for now."

We walk in silence for a few hours until the sun starts to hide behind the horizon. The days aren't long here, which slows us down. I'm guessing she's trying to remember being a jaguar. I couldn't imagine being in her shoes. To have blackouts and wake up with blood on my hands. At least before, she didn't know she was doing it. But now? She has to live with the guilt, and that cannot be easy.

But still, her silence worries me. Every so often, I steal a glance toward her and watch the intensity in her expression. I want to ask her what's on her mind, but I think the better of it. She needs time to process.

As for me, the closer I get to where the Ace of Swords is, the more real it becomes. I lost my mother's runes that got me here, and my hope for finding that sword was to go to Jotunheim. But I'm not leaving without those runes.

"We should make camp. It's getting dark." Kenjō's voice brings me back to the present, and I slow my step.

The twilight sun accentuates Kenjō's features, bringing out the soft glow of her cheeks and her full lips. Long curly strands of her hair stick out from her coat. There's something about the way she looks right now. I mean, to me, she always looks beautiful I had never seen an Ipani before this. But it's something else. Like her eyes have a hint of feline in the way she stares at me. Pretty but dangerous.

But that's not Kenjō. That's just the Rikorō running through her veins.

The real Kenjō is naturally caring, not a ravenous beast. Her sense of humor and caring nature sometimes makes me forget what I'm doing here. She didn't have to save me from the guards; she could have just kept walking. Maybe she doesn't want to be alone after feeling isolated in her treehouse for so long. Either way, I'm glad she did. I was a fool to walk away from her the first time. I never would have made it this far.

Kenjō builds the tent, and I make the fire while Alfred hunts for food. Or at least I try to make the fire. My hands grow tired from rubbing sticks together. What am I doing wrong?

"Do you need my help?" Kenjō's voice carries in the wind.

"Nope, I got it." I am going to get it if it's the last thing I do. I drop the sticks and shake my hands.

"This area is damp. That's probably why you can't get a spark," she says.

I bite my upper lip. She's right. The snow does look like it's melting a bit. I take a deep breath, readying myself to try again. A smile creeps on my face as the image of Aunt Liv surfaces in my mind the day she made the fire while we were camping. That night she told me the rune Kenaz was my mother's rune. Because she loved learning, like the steady kindling of a controlled flame. She told me Kenaz could be mine as well because I'm just like her.

Kenaz, I mouth. Just wanting to feel it as if my mother and Aunt Liv were here with me.

Heat warms my face, and I frown. "Kenjō, I wanted to do it. You've done so much already."

"È? I didn't do anything."

My eyes blink open. "What?" Bright flames dance in the firepit and a red image of the rune Kenaz flashes before my eyes until it disappears in the fumes.

"Harold? You used magic..."

"Without my mother's runes." My jaw drops. "I didn't know that was possible..." Or maybe I can continue using them after I've bonded with them… but I didn't bond with Kenaz. Or did I? I have been pulling it out since I got here, and it does represent my mother, so… I chuckle. Maybe I've always been bonded with Kenaz.

I spring to my feet and jump in the air, letting out a, "Hell yeah! I bonded with Kenaz!"

"Harold, keep it down!"

Alfred jumps to his feet and groans, scanning the area as if we're under attack.

"Sorry, sorry, sorry!" A wide grin spreads on my face, a buzz of excitement entering my spirit. I sit back down despite my sudden need to sprint up a mountain. I cast a look at Kenjō, who's shaking her head smiling and staring at me. If I didn't know any better, she's looking at me with wonderment. Or maybe that's just what I want to be seeing.

"You are so powerful, Harold." Her eyes widen. "You are *naro*. Amazing."

My cheeks burn. "Yeah? You should see me once I get my mother's runes back and bond with the rest of them." Oh, this means I can still use Uruz.

"Be careful using it though, è? We don't want to get caught."

"Fine, fine. I know." Killjoy.

She gets up and disappears into the tent. I stay put next to Alfred and start making little flames on the tip of the stick I had been using before. Kenaz lights up and disappears. I do it over and over. What can I say? I have power, and I want to use it. Alfred stares at me as I do.

I have to be honest. Despite it being incredibly weird having a yeti around, he comes in handy. He even brought his special dome warming potion, so a nice red and warming shield extends past the tent and is keeping our area nice and toasty. I think I'm going to miss the guy after I leave. He's useful, scares predators, and he doesn't talk much. What's not to like?

Kenjō returns with a small vial containing an amber-colored solution.

"What's that?" I ask her.

"You're going to need this." She takes out a coiled rope and spreads it on the ground. She drips a few drops of the solution to one end, and it begins to slither like a snake.

Oh, familiar rope-snake. We meet again.

She hands me the rope, and I eye it in her hand.

"Take it."

I reach to grab it, and it moves. I recoil.

"It won't bite, you know. It doesn't have a mouth."

"Of course, it doesn't." I take the rope from her. "It's a rope."

"Hnn." She watches me with a smirk as I go over to the tree next to where she set up the tent, and I wrap the rope around its bark.

After we eat, I wrap the rope around her torso and around the tree.

"That's not tight enough," she says. "Tighter."

"I don't want to hurt you."

"Tighter."

"Are you sure?"

"Do you want to wake up to me feasting from your stomach?"

I gulp. "No..."

"Then tie it tighter."

"Doesn't it have ouma? I thought it would do the work."

"I just want to make sure."

I place a hand on her shoulder. "I know. It'll be okay. Are you cold?" I reach for the blanket and wrap it around her. Even though the dome is toasty, it's nice to sleep with a blanket, and she's uncomfortable enough as it is being tied to a tree.

"What about you?" She asks.

"I'll be fine. Alfred and I will cuddle." I glance up and give her a half smile. She stares down at me with amusement in her eyes.

Alfred groans behind me, and I chuckle.

"Seriously, I'll be in the tent, and I'll keep the fire going. You're the one who's out here tied up to a tree in the snow."

She leans her head back, and I lie down inside the tent next to her. We positioned it so that she wouldn't be alone. Alfred sprawls out by the fire, staring at the sky. Purple and blue spirals spin in and out of each other among the stars. It's strange to believe that I'm staring at a completely different galaxy in an entirely different dimension.

I lie with my head toward the fire, facing Kenjō. Her eyes are closed, and her knees are drawn in against her chest. The flames dance on her face, enhancing her soft features.

"I've never seen swirls like that before. They're beautiful."

"Yes. How does the sky look where you are from?"

"It's beautiful, vast, like yours. No swirls, though. Hey, how do you say sky in your language?"

"Kenjō," she laughs.

I lift my head. "Really? Your name means sky?"

"Yes, in Ipani. Does Harold mean anything?"

"Um, I think it means messenger." I chuckle. I doubt that's why my parents named me that, though.

"I like it. It's a nice name."

I smile. "I like Kenjō. It's pretty. How do you say pretty in Ipani?"

"Simo."

"Simo," I repeat as I stare at her and think I see a smile on her face through the flickering flames. My eyelids start to grow heavy, and I finally fall asleep.

Sometime through the night, a struggled cry wakes me. I spring up from the tent to find Kenjō has shifted into a jaguar, and the rope is tightening around her head with the rope wedged inside her mouth. Her stomach is turned upright as part of the rope forces her down like a straight jacket. She kicks in protest and then starts to violently struggle with the rope.

Alfred inches toward us, sleepily keeping an eye on her.

"Should I do something? What if it strangles her?" But if I cut the rope, she'll get away. "Kenjō?"

The rope tightens around her head between her mouth. No matter how hard she bites down, instead of the rope breaking, it constricts.

I prop myself up on my elbows. "Kenjō, calm down."

A deep gurgling roar comes from the back of her throat. She pushes the rope with her hind leg as she manages to get it from under its hold. The rope constricts, yanking her upright and flipping her upside down. She cries out in pain and starts to hyperventilate.

Climbing onto my feet, I take out my pocketknife for precaution. "I can't let you loose. I'll never catch you... and you'll eat me."

Alfred groans behind me.

I turn to him. "Be ready, will you? I'm about to do something." What I'm going to do, I have no idea. But I can't leave her like this all night. She'll get hurt. "Okay, Kenjō," I whisper. "Don't bite me."

Her eyes enlarge as I approach her shadow. A growl rumbles from her chest, and I tense my hand. She tries to back up, the rope tightening even more, and she lets out a whimper. Tying her up was a bad idea.

I try to steady my shaking hand as I hold the knife up to her mouth. She told me the enchantment works on what it's meant to constrict, not from the outside, allowing me to slice through it. I place my hand on her head, and she begins to squirm.

"Hold still, Kenjō. I'm trying to help you."

She growls as I press the blade over the rope by the edge of her lips. Her hot breath touches my skin as my fingers brush against her sharp teeth. My heart skips a beat, and I hold my breath. All it takes is for her to chomp down, and I lose my fingers.

My breathing grows heavy as I start slicing the rope. She lifts her head, but I block with my other hand. "Easy now, Kenjō," I whisper. "Just one more, and your mouth will be free."

Her chest pants as I hold her head down and start to stroke the top of her head, cutting quickly. This seems to calm her a bit as she stops squirming, but her tail starts to slap the ground.

"There. Done." I bring my hand back and tuck the knife away. The bottom of the end tightens around her. Me cutting the rope from her mouth wasn't enough to stop it from working entirely—good. She stretches her jaw and squares her eyes on me. Alfred stands behind me, but I hold my hand out. "Wait," I say. "I want to see if she remembers me."

The rope around her torso relaxes as we back off. Her hind legs budge to position underneath her, and the rope grips her, pulling her back. She reaches back to bite the rope.

"Kenjō, don't."

She snaps her gaze to me. Does she remember her name? I glance at Alfred, who's staring at her.

"Kenjō?" I squat down a little closer. "Can you understand me?"

She groans and puts her head down.

I turn to the yeti. "I think I'm getting through to her." He shrugs.

"Kenjō? Can you understand me?" I take a step forward.

She licks her lips and yawns. What does that mean?

"If you can understand me, try shifting back."

She lets out a low whimper.

Cautiously, I take a seat beside her head. We keep an eye on each other as I sit down and slowly place my hand on her head. She flinches at first but then leans into my hand. I start scratching behind her ears, and she closes her eyes. My lips curl into a smile. I don't know if she's going to remember this in the morning, but I don't think I can let her live it down.

Kenjō turns her nose to face me and starts slowly crawling toward my lap, the rope tightening slightly. She pauses and stares at me, so I inch closer until she can reach my legs and places her head on my thighs. My eyes widen, and I glance at Alfred. He huffs and lays back down. I put my hand on her head and start to stroke her fur. "You're okay, Kenjō. You're figuring it out."

Her nose wiggles, and her ear moves toward the sound of my voice. I keep stroking her fur down to her neck. The flames flicker in front of us, and my eyes grow heavy. My eyes close, but I keep stroking her fur. Her paws close on the side of my thighs, and suddenly I feel fingers as the fur between my hands turns to hair. I open my eyes to Kenjō having turned back into her Ipani self. She sniffles and starts to shake as her voice turns into sobs.

"Are you okay?" I ask.

She shakes her head. Her eyes are squeezed shut as she cries. She grips my clothes between her fingers. "I killed them. Those were my people, and I killed them."

I wrap my arms around her and bring her head up to my chest. "Shh… It wasn't you."

"Yes, it was."

"You didn't know what you were doing."

"I hurt so many. It's all my fault." She cries. "I should never have used the Rikorō on myself."

I sigh deeply. I can't believe I'm about to say this. "You didn't want to hurt a kidnapped Ipani anymore than they already had been, Kenjō. You did what you thought was right."

"And now, I'm going to die because of it."

My stomach sinks. "No. You're going to use the Rikorō to make the healing potion. I know you'll find a way." I lift up her chin, "look at me." Tears roll down her wet cheeks, and the soft gleam from the dying fire reflecting on her pupils makes her look more like a cat's, even in this form. "I won't let you die, Kenjō. We're going to figure it out, okay?"

She props herself up and wipes her eyes.

"And you know what?"

"What?"

"You're still wearing clothes."

She gasps and clutches her coat. I laugh. Yeah, that would have been awkward. "How did that happen?"

She laughs, coughing at the end as she dries her eyes. "I heard of Ipani wearing their clothes in the Aō after eating an aetochi."

"A what?"

"A cookie but made with *solerie* to become like a ghost. Like a specter.

"A magical cookie that can turn you invisible?"

She nods.

"So what, you can keep your clothes on you?"

"As long as you think it, you can will it. I must have been conscious about them."

"It looked like you were starting to remember. That's progress."

"Yes. I remembered... a lot of things." Her voice cracks.

"It's going to be okay."

She yawns, and the rope tightens around her waist. "I just wanted to be useful. I wanted to prove to my mom I can match up to her standards."

"You were just doing what you were told, Kenjō. You were put in an impossible situation." A morally messed up one. She was told to believe the ends justify the means.

All she was doing was listening to her mother. Doing what her mother wanted her to do even though this wasn't her path. Even for someone as independent as Kenjō, living and hunting on her own. She was ready to defend herself, and to die before she killed another, even though that backfired, she didn't want to hurt someone else. She never should have listened to her mom. They told her it was to save their kind, but it's the wrong way.

She backs into the rope so that it gives her some slack, and I glance at her. "Do you think you'll turn again?"

"I don't know."

I pull out my pocketknife. "I'm willing to take the chance. You're showing progress."

"Are you sure?"

"Well," I get up and stick the blade under the rope, cutting her free. "If not, we'll pay the price later."

"Thank you."

I give her a smile. "Let's sleep." I get up and walk back to the tent with her following behind me. As I lay my head down to rest, she pulls the blanket up and climbs in next to me. My breath hitches as she snuggles up to me.

Well, I'm not going to protest.

She turns around, making me wrap my arms around her. My muscles tense. I've never done this before. It's... nice. I allow myself to relax as I move her hair from her face and stroke her cheek. I wonder if she realizes how much she risked in trying to save the other Ipani by not experimenting on them. Sure, she wanted ouma. But did she know she was sacrificing her life? She knew the Rikorō was dangerous; she told me it's killing her. Deep inside, she had to have known. I tuck a loose strand of her behind her ear.

After a few moments, I lay my head back down and go to sleep, thinking about what I would do to save my aunt from dying from the curse. So far, I've set my heart to going to Jotunheim and trying to plead my case to the Frost Giants. But what if I never make it? What if I can't make a sacrifice for the Ace of Swords to work for me? What if I never retrieve my mother's runes?

All would be lost, and all this would have been for nothing. My aunt would die not knowing what happened to me... If worse comes to worst, and I cannot make it to Jotunheim, I might have to enact my aunt's curse on me. But that would mean the only way to save my aunt would be for me to kill...

CHAPTER FOURTEEN

C OLD WIND JERKS ME AWAKE. I SQUINT UP AT A LFRED holding the tent above our heads, eclipsing the bright sunlight behind him. With a loud growl, he throws the tent against a tree.

"What the hell?' I sit up, and Kenjō rubs her eyes, the warmth between us having kept us comfortable all night. I smile inwardly despite my annoyance. "Why did you do that?"

Alfred groans.

"There are nicer ways of waking us up, you know."

Kenjō laughs. "Not to him."

"How about some breakfast?" I say to him, kicking the blanket off my feet. "Make yourself useful."

"He has been useful," Kenjō says.

"I know. But still, he didn't have to throw our tent—er, your tent."

She blushes and starts to gather her belongings. "We need to go."

I wipe my face. "Did we sleep through the morning?"

The yeti huffs.

"Okay, I get it. You're bored. We aren't holding you. You can go home."

The yeti's brows furrow as he stares at me then looks to Kenjō and huffs.

"I think he likes our company," she says, folding the tent into a tight square. "Besides, he can keep us safe while we journey to the spirit forest."

"Fine." I climb to my feet and push past him, giving him a side-eye. "Let's be on our way then. Stop throwing stuff around."

He groans at me.

I groan at him right back, and he stops to stare at me. I suppress a laugh. Feels like I'm traveling with a Wookie.

"What is with you two?" Kenjō walks between us, taking the lead. "Come on, it's late."

"He started it." I follow her out of the woods and up a field of snowy rolling hills. We walk for miles with the snow up to our knees; the only solace is a breath-taking view of the snowy mountain peaks we're walking toward. They're almost as beautiful as Kenjō.

As we walk in silence, a knot forms in my stomach. Not the knot I've gotten used to ever since my mom passed and continues to grow as I find new ways I could enact my curse. That knot is still there.

This is a new kind of knot that twists every time Kenjō looks at me or talks to me. Last night I forced myself to sleep to keep myself from reaching over to kiss her. What if she doesn't want me to?

I knew I found her attractive, but this is the first time I admit to myself that I like her. This is dumb. After I find my mother's runes and leave, I'll probably never see her again.

My throat closes up.

A haunting moan is carried by the wind. I pause and turn to face Alfred. "Did you say something?"

He shakes his head.

"It's coming from the forest," Kenjō says. "We are close."

Worry lines wrinkle her forehead. I recall her telling me the forest is haunted, but it didn't compute that haunted here could mean... actual ghosts. No wonder she didn't want to go in.

We keep walking until we reach a clearing before a dark forest. Twisted thorn bushes surround dead trees. The winds from the mountain have died down, and a strange eerie quiet settles around us. A different kind of cold reaches my bones.

"We're here." She whispers.

"This is the spirit forest?" A tortured scream breaks the silence, and I jump.

She nods. "This is it." She takes a step back.

"Hey, it's okay. We'll stick together." I reach my hand out to her. "How far in do you think we have to go for your plant?"

"It doesn't matter. The temple that protects the sword is outside the forest."

I squint my eyes through the thick trees and branches, shrouding a dense shade, giving the allure that it's nighttime. I try to see the light at the far end but don't. How far do these woods stretch? I cast a look at Kenjō, who's unstrapping her spear from her back and gripping it tightly in her hand. She bites her upper lip as she stares into the woods. "Ready?" I ask.

Kenjō peers into the forest. "No, but let's get it over with."

Alfred groans loudly.

"You coming?" I ask him. Alfred's brows furrow hard as he stares into the dead trees, hesitant to take a step.

"Out here, the Aō and this plane become one. He senses it." Kenjō says as she approaches the yeti. "This is where we part ways. Thank you for keeping us safe inside your Aō dome."

Alfred groans and she gives him a hug. He releases her embrace and stares at me.

Giving him a half hug, I say, "I'm glad to have met you. Take care, big guy."

He groans once and watches as we leave him behind to head inside the dead forest. I take Kenjō's hand, and she startles at first. But then closes her hand around mine.

"We got this," I tell her.

We take the first steps into the forest at the same time. Snow glistens on the barks of the dead trees. The dry air presses against my cheeks as I search the area. "This isn't so bad."

We walk up and down hills amid the snowy trees and shrubs with Kenjō still clutching my hand.

A shadow zooms above us, and she ducks. I turn to see where it went, but it disappears. Another shadow zooms past us and disappears into a tree. Kenjō walks closer to me, her arm pressing against mine.

"Just keep your eyes straight ahead," I reassure her.

A shadow looms above us, and I try my best to ignore it. "Kenjō?" I whisper. "These... are just spirits, right? They can't hurt us?"

She stares at me and parts her lips.

I blink a few times. "Can they hurt us?"

"If they grab us, they can drag us underground."

Where we'd suffocate and die. Frigg. "Let's not get caught then." We clutch our hands together and keep walking deeper into the woods, my eyes peeled for any hints of plants that can be Rikorō—even though I have no idea what that plant looks like.

As our feet crunch on the snow, I'm hyper-sensitive to our surroundings. My hair rises at any noise, even from our own footsteps. Keep it together, Harold.

The sound of someone crying somewhere in the forest makes Kenjō stop.

What is she doing.

"It sounds like a woman," she whispers.

"It sounds like a spirit. Which means we shouldn't go looking for it."

She sniffs the air as if her jaguar self is merging with her Ipani self and starts walking off toward the right.

Odin's balls. "Where are you going?" I run after her. She ignores me.

So much for staying on task.

Shadows pass over our heads, and I duck, looking up as I walk. Kenjō keeps a brisk pace, robotically following the sounds of crying.

"I don't like this," I tell her.

She stops abruptly and points to a blackened, dead tree with no leaves on it. "Look over there." I glance at the tree while still being cautious of the shadows flying over our heads. The vine starts from the bottom, making its way up the tree's bark. Thorns with red tips wrap around it. "That's Rikorō."

I gape at it. "Looks friendly."

She chuckles and walks over, taking off her satchel and opening it to grab another three vials inside her leather sample booklet. She selects medium-sized ones and grips her knife, and starts cutting the vine.

I approach it carefully, not wanting to prick my skin on one of those red-tipped edges. "So, this is the soul-eater, huh?"

"Yes."

"How do you use it?"

"I extract the sap from the vine."

Interesting. My eyes follow the vine all the way to the top of the tree and stop at some of its flowering sprouts. The petals are long and blood-red, like its thorns. "Do you do anything with the flower?"

"I will take some too, to experiment. I have never seen it growing before," she says. "The forager usually only brings me the vine." She pauses. "Or... used to."

I'll shut up now.

A loud, jarring scream erupts in my eardrums, and something wraps itself around my calf. I jump back but fall on my rear. I gape at my leg as a rotting hand clutches its long curled fingernails around my legs, piercing my pants. I let out a hoarse yelp and kick at it with my other foot, pulling myself back. A pair of hands emerge from the snow next to me and grab my arms, pulling me down. I'm lying flat against my back as I squirm left to right. "Kenjō!"

Kenjō jumps to me, her mouth gaping. She takes the knife and swings it over her head,

"No!" I yell, afraid she might accidentally cut my leg off.

She swings down hard, taking the hand off its arm. I kick

free, but the hands still grip my shoulders. More arms stick up from the ground and tug on my clothes, pulling me down. One presses down on my chest.

Kenjō cuts at them rapidly, but more come up and pull me down until I can no longer move my limbs. She drops the knife and frantically grabs at their bones, trying her hardest to free me.

The ground starts to loosen under me, and as a hand covers my eyes and mouth, the smell of its rotting flesh infesting my nostrils, I cry out, but my voice is muffled.

The snow covers my body completely, and the icy ground below the surface opens. I swallow snow on my way down, struggling to breathe.

"Harold!" Kenjō's voice sounds distant, being overpowered by the pounding cries of the dead trying to take me with them. My legs and arms stiffen as something wraps around me tighter, pulling me further down.

Something digs above me. At least I think there's digging, but I don't know how much longer I can hold my breath. I shake violently, trying to shake off the dead, trying to get them to let go. Loud groans escape me as I can no longer open my mouth to let out a scream. But at this point, I don't think anyone above ground can hear me.

Panic pounds at my chest. I can't move my arms and legs. I can't crawl my way out. Cold soil enters my mouth, and my chest aches from holding my breath.

I can't hold it anymore.

Soil and snow rush up my nostrils, and a searing pain bursts through my temples and ears. My body tries to cough as I suffocate.

I can't think.

I'm too far down. I won't make it.

My aunt's voice hijacks my mind. *Trust the runes.*

Aunt Liv?

The memory of me being so frightened I summoned Uruz to attack the jaguar resurfaces. But... I'm scared, and I don't feel the runes. I don't have them. I can't...

A chunk of soil gets lodged in my throat as I find a small pocket of air. My chest convulses with urges to regurgitate.

Uruz

The voice rings in my head as if my aunt were here with me. I need to get out. I need to save her.

I think of the rune, lit up red in the center of my mind. I will its power to course through my veins. I guess that's enough because my arms vibrate, followed by my entire body. *"Uruz."* An image of the rune rushes through my mind, or at least I think it's in my mind because the ground opens.

My eyes burst open, and I'm lunged out of the ground. I grip onto the edge of what now looks like a crater and cough as my lungs open and I gasp for air. Dirt regurgitates from my throat as my chest heaves furiously. I glance up at Kenjō in jaguar form as fleshy bones claw at her body. She grabs them between sharp teeth and shakes them apart like a ragdoll.

An arm springs from under the ground and grabs my neck, squeezing hard. I clutch its rotten wrist and mutter the rune, "Kenaz." The hand bursts into flames and drops to the ground. I turn to help Kenjō, who's still struggling to get away from the tortured dead.

Kenjō shakes her entire body furiously, then leaps past me in an abrupt attempt to get away.

I quickly grab her satchel and dash after her. Despite her being ten times faster than me, I don't try to call after her. I follow her tracks until she stops at a lake covered in ice.

Her body shakes as she starts to shift back to her Ipani form. Her leather coat suddenly materializes over her jaguar arms as she shifts back. I'll never get used to that.

My chest is still heaving. "Let's never do that again," I say between winded breaths.

"Are you alright?" She pats herself down to make sure her clothes are still on, and she's still in one piece. Which they are, and she is.

Without saying a word, I go to her and pull her into me. She startles for a moment but then wraps her arms around my waist. She pulls away and touches my cheek with her hand. "I thought you were dead. I tried to dig to reach you, but..."

"It's okay. I had to remember my aunt and my mom were with me the entire time." I smile. She smiles back with her brows furrowed. I know she doesn't understand, but that's okay. I needed to remember who I was. I let her go and handed her satchel back to her. "Were you able to collect what you needed from the Rikorō before I was abducted by dead things?"

Kenjō nods, "I was, thankfully."

"Let's get out of here. This place gives me the creeps." A tiny spot of blood drips from her nose. "Kenjō, you're bleeding."

She gasps and quickly wipes it away.

I scan our surrounding area. This isn't ideal, but... "should we stop and rest?" If she feels bad, I don't want her passing out, especially if it's due to the poisonous plant.

"No, I will be fine."

I purse my lips and stare at her, unsure if she's telling the truth or pretending to be strong. "But you're bleeding."

"It's just a little blood, like before. I feel fine, I promise. We'll rest when we leave."

"Fine, but if you start to feel bad, we need to stop."

She wipes her face one more time and secures her ponytail. "We are going to Alec's tower after, è? I will ask him for a ride back to mine with one of his soldiers so that I get home quicker. He won't say no to me."

My gut clenches at the mention of Alec. But, with a deep breath, I let it go. At least she'll have someone to get her home quickly before the Rikorō takes her. I don't want to think about that last part. "We have to hurry so you can get to making that cure."

She reaches for my hand, and we start to walk side by side, keeping an eye out for the tortured spirits. A hauntingly beautiful voice serenades the air with a song.

Kenjō pauses.

Her singing stops, and after a few easy breaths, we walk again.

"*Kenjō?*" The spirit's voice reappears.

Kenjō gasps and stops in her tracks. We turn to face the image of a woman in a long white dress. The image flickers in front of us. She has long, wavy dark hair, dark round eyes, and cheekbones akin to Kenjō's. The resemblance is uncanny.

Oh no. "Kenjō, come on. We have to go, remember?"

"She knows my name...What if she's my mother?"

"Kenjō..." I stop myself. What would I do if I saw my

mother's spirit? I wouldn't be able to ignore her. But what if she's no longer Kenjō's mom and means us harm?

The spirit of a woman floats in front of us. She extends her hand out to Kenjō. Kenjō's eyes well up, and she lifts her hand up to touch her. "Mother..."

What would happen if they touched? It could grab her and drag her down like the others tried to do to me. I place my arm around Kenjō's shoulder and try to lead her away.

Kenjō lets the woman touch her cheek. Nothing happens, and I relax my shoulders. It really is her mom.

"Mother..." Kenjō's voice shakes as tears start flowing down her cheeks. I back away, giving them some space.

What would I do to get a moment with my mom again? Kenjō never met her biological mother before this. Goes to show a mother will always recognize her child.

Kenjō's mother smiles down at her daughter. "Kenjō... this is not right. Your ouma... It isn't right."

"I know, Mother." Her voice is shaky, heavy with sadness. She stares at her mom, and I know what she's thinking. How can she make this moment last?

The ground shakes around us, and rotten hands rip from the ground, reaching to grab at our legs.

"Kenjō..." I start to tug on her shoulder. "We have to go."

The bodies start to lift from the surface, pulling themselves up. For miles, the dead lift themselves up. Some still have their leathery flesh hanging from their bones, and others are missing half their faces. A few dozen are full skeletons. And they are facing us, coming after us.

"Go, Harold." She says without looking at me.

I gape at her. "What are you talking about?"

"This is what guards Naó. That is why they were buried here. They don't want you to reach the sword. Go now. I'll stay behind to fend them off."

"Hell no. I'm not leaving you here to die."

She turns to me. "I'm fine. I'm with my mom."

"Kenjō, you have to come with me. You'll die here and become one of them." I reach to touch her sleeve, but she pulls away from me.

"At least I'll be with her." She stares back at her mom. "I don't want to leave."

The army of dead surrounds us. Their bones bend and crack as they slowly make their way toward us. I ready myself to call upon Uruz again, but that might blast her mom too. I might not have a choice. I stare at her mom. "She can't stay here. You know that, right?"

Her mother snaps her gaze to me. "Kenjō can do what she wants."

CHAPTER FIFTEEN

Her mother's spirit places her hand on Kenjō's face, ignoring the marching dead coming after us.

I steady my hands, my eyes shifting between the ghost and the walking dead. Their cries and tortured moans ring in my ears.

Soft white hues emanate from Kenjō's mother's aura. As a cold wind blows her hair, she looks down at her daughter. "You have grown to be a beautiful young woman who is learning to be wise. I could not be prouder." She smiles warmly at her. "But Kenjō, if you stay here, you will become part of the tortured dead, forever. Please make the decision to leave this place and never return."

I lower my hands. I really did not want to blast her mother. But there was no way I was going to let Kenjō die.

"But I just got you back," Kenjō's voice cracks.

"I can see you are far stronger than I ever was. And you will continue to be. Leave now, take care of yourself. Never return."

Her mother turns toward the surrounding dead and lets out a loud wail. I close my ears with my hands and ready myself to run as the dead startle and back up.

"Wait—" Kenjō reaches toward her mother, who turns around. "I—I thought you were part of them. Part of the tortured..."

Her mother's eyes grow solemn. "My remains are forever in pain, alive and half dead, as is my soul. But my greatest pain was never knowing you."

Kenjō lets out a sob.

The dead start to walk toward us again, their bones creaking and unhinging as they move.

"When I felt you near," her mother says. "I was able to collect pieces of myself long enough to see you, but my time is growing short. Go now, while I am still strong enough to fend them off. Go!"

The tortured dead block our way out. I grab onto Kenjō's arm, and this time she lets me pull her away.

Her mother unhinges her jaw as she stares at the dead behind her. I wince in anticipation of my bleeding ears. She lets out a long siren wail. Power emanates from her scream, sending many of the tortured to fall on their backs. Now, we both turn to run but are blocked by more dead behind us.

"Uruz!" The wild ox emanates from my chest and stampedes the dead behind us. They fall to the ground, but in seconds I know they'll be back up. We run through their bones as they reach for us.

Kenjō reaches back and pulls her spear from its strap, swinging it sharply in front of her and decapitating a skeleton.

We pick up speed and sprint through the path with twisted

dead trees, careful not to stumble on a root hidden beneath the snow. Out through the trees, soft orangey light peeks from the edge of the forest. We don't stop to look back; we run fast until we're out of the woods.

I stop at the edge of the forest and grip my knees, panting hard. Kenjō reaches for her canteen inside her satchel and takes a long swig before handing it to me. "Do we... have to... go through that on the way...back?" I say, trying to catch my breath.

She shakes her head. "No, it was only to collect the Rikorō. On the way back, we'll walk against the coast to the Prefect's Tower."

Right. So, either face the tortured dead or face the Prefect and the Arcana soldiers. Noted.

Kenjō gazes out toward the dark woods of the spirit forest. The twisted branches of the dead trees cast dark shadows on the ground. She clutches her satchel so hard her knuckles are turning white.

I place my hand on her shoulder. "Are you okay?"

She takes a deep breath and lets it out slowly. "I'm okay."

We can't do anything about her mother's eternal torture. But the fact that she got to see her, and got a chance to say goodbye, is so much more than anyone can ask for. Her mother said her greatest pain was never knowing Kenjō. Maybe now, some of her pain would be put to rest. Perhaps there was a greater purpose for entering the spirit forest other than getting the Rikorō.

We stand there a few minutes longer, letting the harrowing moans carry through the wind. She's waiting to see if her mom appears at the edge of the woods, and I don't want to rush her. When no one comes, she turns to face me.

"Thank you for not leaving me there," she says.

I blink a few times. "Leave you? I would never do that."

"But I told you to. You need the sword to retrieve your magic. To break your family's curse, è? My burden is not yours to bear. Anyone else would have left."

My lips part, and I stare into her eyes; they glisten with tears forming at the bridge. "Kenjō," I say in almost a whisper. "Making sure you live *is* my burden to bear." And it's not because I'm afraid that I might enact my curse if she dies. I do not want her to die either way, especially not by being taken by the tortured dead. And the kind of "death" this world brings? I wouldn't wish it on anyone. I swallow a lump forming in my throat. "I care about you."

She sucks in a breath and bites her lower lip. Despite the cold air, my cheeks warm. I should have stayed quiet. Frigg. A smile creeps on her face, and she looks down, trying to hide her rosy cheeks. I bite down a laugh. "Shall we get going?" I ask.

"Yes."

The sun is setting over the horizon of the vast mountains. "How far is the Temple from here?"

"It should be half a day's journey, but it is getting dark. Why don't we get farther away from the woods to make camp?"

"And get away from the cries of tortured dead? Don't twist my arm."

She casts me a confused glare, and I laugh to myself.

"It's a good idea," I say. "But maybe tomorrow you should

head to Alec's Tower, and I'll continue on my mission myself. You need to work on your cure."

Her face pales as she stops to stare at me. "You don't want me to come with you?"

"Oh, I—I didn't mean it that way. But you need to cure yourself, Kenjō. You got your plant. You can leave."

"The next wooded area should be right outside Naó. We have a long way to go on just snowy planes. But," she takes out a small vial with a red solution. "We still have enough heating potion from the grotto."

"Kenjō..."

"Naó is going to be guarded. You'll need my help as a jaguar. You helped me and stayed in the forest with me, Harold. I won't leave you alone now. Or, what if I collapse from the Rikorō on the way to Alec's and I'm by myself, è?"

I scratch the back of my head. Fair enough. "Aren't we a little visible?"

She smiles. "Out here? We are far enough from civilization that no one will spot us past the spirit forest."

"That's good enough for me."

We walk side by side down the rolling hills covered in snow. Step one—retrieving the supremely illegal plant is complete. I just hope she really can make that cure. At least no one's gotten hurt. Now, all I have to do is execute steps two and three—get the sword, get Alec to do what I say, and I'm on my way to get my mother's runes back. Then, goodbye Piupeki and Tarotland. I glimpse at Kenjō, who's deep in thought, staring down at the snow as she walks. Maybe there's a chance I can come back someday.

We walk alongside each other until we're far enough away

from the spirit forest to not be bothered by its eerie cries. Around us, a few trees and shrubs are scattered. It's not a densely wooded area, but at least it isn't totally empty, snowy plains like she suspected. The temperature's now dropped since the sun is completely gone.

"You make the fire, and I will hunt," she says.

"The fire will take me a second," with my newfound power. "I can help you hunt."

Kenjō takes off her satchel and leans it against a tree. The corner of her lips curls into a smirk as she unbuttons her coat and lays it on top of her satchel. I squint at her. "What are you going to do?"

Her smirk turns into a full-on smile, and her arms and legs begin to shift.

I cross my arms in front of me. "Show off."

She makes a circle and lets out a soft purring sound.

"Guess that makes it easier to hunt." Makes me wish I could turn into an animal.

She takes off running deep into the woods, leaving me alone to my fire duties. Hey, making fires are important too. It's cold out. I get to work on clearing an area, using her spear, and finding the stones and wood.

Once I've whispered the rune, Kenaz, the fire is ablaze. I reach into her satchel and find the yeti's superheating dome solution. After pouring a few drops into the fire and watching the red sphere be cast from the flames and into a perfect dome suitable for Kenjō and me, I build the tent and make it nice and cozy. I lay on my back and let the heat warm me as I watch the purple and blue swirls of the night sky move in a nautilus dance above the dome.

A rustling comes from behind me, but I assume it's Kenjō and ignore it. A few minutes pass, and Kenjō hasn't stepped out from there.

Now, I sit up. "Kenjō? Is that you?" Another rustling comes but now from the bushes to my right. I climb to my feet and peer into the bushes, then the woods, my shadow eclipsing the light from the fire behind me.

My hairs stand on end. It's been more than an hour since Kenjō went hunting. She's usually faster than this on foot. As a jaguar, she should be even faster. Unless she started playing with her food. Which would mean the jaguar took over. I gulp. I hope to Odin she hasn't reverted back. Could that happen?

"Kenjō?" I move the leaves from the bushes to the side, searching the ground.

Footsteps creep up from behind, and I spin around to see large white teeth and the jaguar they belong to, ready to pounce.

With no time to move out of the way, my instincts kick in. I lift my arms in front of me and scream like a girl.

Kenjō's paws weigh down on my shoulders as she leaps, knocking me on my back. My heart shoots up to my throat, hammering so loud it reverberates in my ears.

"Kenjō..."

Her weight presses against me with her paws pinning my shoulders down and the rest of her body blocking me from standing. I try to nudge her, but she's solid as a rock. I close my eyes, and I wait for her to sink her teeth in. When she doesn't, I open my eyes. She's staring at me straight in the face, her breath hot against my cheek. Her form starts to shift back.

"Kenjō?"

She grins mischievously and stares at me with a glint in her eye.

"You're kidding."

She starts laughing uncontrollably, and I start to get up, but her hands are still holding my shoulders as she straddles me with her legs.

"That wasn't funny. I thought you reverted back to pure jaguar." Her tight black tunic sticks to the form of her curves, her hair pouring over her shoulders, touching her elbows.

"You should have seen your face," she laughs. "You were so scared."

"Of course, I was." I clear my throat.

"You thought I was going to eat you."

"Well, yeah. But also, I was afraid you lost all the progress you made, and it would be it. Even if you wouldn't have eaten me, Kenjō. You could have run off, and I'd never see you again."

This makes her stop smiling. "You were afraid of me losing myself?"

"Obviously," I say, fully aware of her still being on top of me. The fire illuminates the right side of her face, and she lowers her eyes at me.

"I am sorry."

"It's okay. You were joking."

She stares at me intently, and I stare back at her, adamantly trying to stare at her face and keep my eyes from wandering down.

"If everything goes to your plan tomorrow, you will be on your way to get your magic," she says. "And then you will go home."

"If the Empress doesn't kill me first."

"That won't happen, è? I won't let her."

"Oh?" I smile, propping myself up on my elbow. "And you will stop her?"

"Yes," she smirks. "Even if it means making more Rikorō so that I overpower her."

I frown. "No, Kenjō. Not like that. You'll kill yourself."

"I won't. But I will help you find your magic."

I slant my smile again, brushing her face with the back of my fingers. "You little convict." What was that? 50 shades of Harold? I bite down a laugh. Not that I'd ever read that. She sucks in a breath at my touch, and I let my fingers brush her bottom lip. What am I doing?

She leans in closer. I suck in a breath and hold it. Her hair falls over her face, covering her eyes, and I pull it back behind her pointy ear, letting my breath out slowly. The red reflection of the dome plus the fire makes her eyes look both fierce yet warm at the same time. Like compassion mixed with curiosity. It makes me want to touch her even more.

I sit myself up slightly and lift her chin, my eyes dipping to her lips. They part, showing the tips of her pointy incisors. I inch my face closer and press my lips against hers. My eyes close as her soft lips warm mine. Then I pull back.

"I'm sorry, Kenjō, I—" My gaze drops to her tongue.

She licks her lips, her eyes still closed, and her breath hitches.

She leans in and kisses me with full force. I sit up, pulling her legs up around me so that we're both sitting up. I cup her face with my hand, taking in her lips. I cannot believe this is happening. I spin her around, laying her body on the ground near the fire. Staring into her dark eyes, I find gold specs reflecting from the blaze behind us. So beautiful. I kiss her neck gently, and she giggles, caressing my back muscles with her fingers. I tense at her touch, her fingernails sending a tickling sensation down my spine. I kiss her chin, making my way up to her lips again.

She smiles into my face, and I smile back, twining her hair between my fingers, then gripping her hair by its roots and pulling gently. A soft moan escapes her mouth as she arches into me, and I catch her lips; I want to keep tasting her.

Her hands wander beneath my shirt. Goosebumps emerge on my skin with her sensual touch as she wanders her fingertips over my pecs. I take off my shirt, and she stares at me, hunger in her eyes as she looks me up and down.

This is really happening.

She leans in and takes my lips into her own. This time she nibbles on my bottom lips. Heat floors inside me, and I find my hands wandering under her tight shirt, caressing her perfect skin, wanting her clothes to come off. I lean down and start kissing her stomach, making my way down.

"Harold..." she whispers, curling her fingers through my hair.

"Mmm?"

"If you didn't have a curse to break," she breathes heavily. "Would you stay with me?"

I glance up at her and make my way back up to her lips. "If I didn't have a curse to break, I'd stay with you forever."

She slips her slender hand down my pants, and I suck in a sharp breath. Standing up, I lift her so she's straddling me as I carry her off into the tent.

CHAPTER SIXTEEN

"IT'S WICKED HOT IN HERE."

Kenjō laughs at my sudden outburst. But really, though, between our body heat and that wonderful heat dome over the tent, I'm sweating my balls off. For the first time since landing in what's apparently the Alaska of Ipa, I'm looking forward to some snow.

I turn over and trace the curves of her body with my fingers. Time is pressing down on me, but I don't want to leave. I wish we could stay this way forever. "What do you think will happen to your jaguar abilities when you make the cure?"

"If I can make it," she corrects.

"When."

She shakes her head. "If the Rikorō leaves my body, it will probably flush out the ouma completely. I won't be able to shift anymore."

My frown deepens. "I'm sorry. I know how much you're enjoying it." Especially now that she can control it and not wake up with blackouts, having eaten half her village.

"It is life. Better to be alive than to die from a poisonous plant, è?"

I lean in and kiss her. "That's exactly what I wanted to hear." I hold her tight, taking in the scent of her hair. My chest tightens as the thought of me having to make a sacrifice to pick up that sword comes to mind. I've been pushing the thoughts of the sacrifice out of my mind because I knew no matter what, I was going to have to figure it out. But the more I spend time with Kenjō, the more it hits me that my sacrifice is going to be leaving her behind. I really don't want to.

But I have to. Breaking my family's curse is my priority, above everything else. Every day I've been here, my aunt has been closer to death due to that curse, and only I can save her. I know it's going to kill me to have to leave Kenjō, but if that sword is the only way to get my mother's runes back and get the portal to open, I have to take it.

But that doesn't mean I can't enjoy the short time I have left with her while I'm here.

Snow starts to fall as we quickly pack up and make our way up the peaks of the forested hills. Every now and then, I turn around and get a glimpse of Rutavenye, the Tower appearing from between the clouds. I'll get up there somehow. I will get my mother's runes back.

We walk for a few miles up the mountain, and at one point, I become distracted enough from looking back at the floating island that I lose sight of Kenjō. I don't know if it was when I was trying to glimpse at the floating island or if she left to use a tree, but I know her well enough to know she wasn't abducted. This was intentional. A smile curls on my lips. "Kenjō?" What mischief is she up to now? I swear she's more like Loki than I'd like to admit. I like it.

A snowball plows against my shoulder, cold bits hitting my ear. "Ow!" I spin around. Kenjō runs up to a fresh pile of snow and starts gathering it in her hands. A wide smile stretches on her face.

"Oh no, you don't," I spin around to do the same, gathering as much snow as I can.

She throws another but this time I duck, and it hits the tree behind me. I launch one at her, and it hits her on the thigh. She laughs and grabs another snowball.

"Just don't use one of your smoke bombs this time!" I say.

She laughs and takes off her satchel.

I throw another one at her, then another in sequence. They hit her square in the chest and neck.

Her eyes widen, and she wipes her face and neck. I back up, readying myself with another snowball. She takes three in her hands and lunges at them, missing only once.

I swing my arm back, aim at her and throw. Just as my snowball lands, she shifts into a jaguar and leaps away.

"Hey, that's not fair!" I quickly grab her satchel but stop for a moment to tie the belt holding her smoke-screen bombs around my belt to keep them from breaking.

She runs at me full speed and skids to a halt, causing a wave of snow to spray my face. Wow. I spit out snow.

"This means war, you know!"

She's already halfway up the path as I try to make another snowball as fast as I can. I run toward the direction she ran off in, but now I don't see her. She's probably hiding up a tree, waiting to pounce.

Slowing my step, I search the canopy, trying to see her black spots and gold fur. "You know I'll find you. You're not exactly a snow leopard. You're easy to spot."

Something jumps down behind me, and I spin around to meet her, placing one stealthy foot in front of the other.

"You're getting good at that," I bounce a snowball on my gloved hand, smile, and lunge it at her torso, but miss and get her ear. Oops.

She hisses at me and flicks snow at my face.

"Sorry!" I laugh. Just when I think she's about to run at me again, she backs up, a low growl escaping her mouth.

My brows furrow. "What is it?"

She starts to shift back, seriousness settling on her face as she fully emerges. She points up to the sky, and I turn around. White gusts of smoke whistle down as Arcana soldiers land miles down the path. "What do you think they're doing?"

"We are not supposed to be up this far," she says out of breath. "We should hurry."

I swallow. "If they knew we were here, they'd come straight for us, wouldn't they? Why land over there?" I turn to look at her and gasp. Blood is dripping from her nose, and her eyes are bloodshot, with bags underneath them. "Kenjō, your nose." I reach into her bag, pull out a rag, and hand it to her. "You're looking a little pale. Are you feeling okay?"

"I'm fine," she says, taking the rag from me and wiping it under her nose.

I arch a brow at her. "Are you sure?"

"I'm the same as always. The sooner we get to the Ace of Swords, the sooner we can get to the Prefect's Tower without being seen." She tugs at my sleeve. Another two sharp whistling sounds land behind us, and I turn to squint at them. Those look and sound uncomfortably closer. She's right; we have to hurry.

Maybe Demitri or Alec lost sight of us and started to track us. For all they know, I was collecting a plant and should be on my way back to their village by now. Time's running out.

"Naó is just over this hill, look." She points to a stone rooftop poking out from the snow-covered trees. "Just a bit further."

As we hike up the mountain, the grounds become more forested. I'm just relieved this forest isn't swarming with the walking dead. Tall stone temple ruins finally greet us. I take in the breathtaking craftsmanship of the two-story building. Within the stonework, etches of symbols and sword fighting Ipani decorate the stone faces. Large pillars lay broken on the ground, evidence of some kind of war. The entrance to the temple is missing its door, but the rest of the building is still intact.

I peer inside the entrance as I take my first steps onto the stone stairs. Kenjō stumbles next to me, and I squint at her. Her face is definitely paler. I hold out my hand, and she takes it, regaining her balance. She gives me a reassuring smile, and we step through the entrance together.

Slivers of light shine down from arched windows at the top. Open corridors wrap around the second floor, letting us see the high ceilings of the temple. A few broken pieces of the cracked ceiling crumble down as we step further inside.

Across the room are four steps leading up to a podium. I squint to the mantle, where a single card is floating upright at the top. I don't see a sword anywhere.

"Where's the sword?"

"I think it is that card," she says.

I arch a brow and take a few steps toward it. Something looms overhead, and I duck. "Isn't there supposed to be something guarding the temple?" We exchange a glance, and both slowly move our gaze to what's looming above us. Kenjō gasps and unstraps her spear.

A black and white striped flying serpent, big enough to swallow me whole with one gulp, sweeps the ceiling. It has black gill-like fins and shimmery gray swirls. Its cruel eyes stare down at me. "What the hell is that?"

"A drakon," she yells.

"A what?"

"This one's mean. Run!" She takes off in a full sprint toward the exit of the temple, and I run after her, jumping over debris from the stone ruins. The drakon swoops down, opens its mouth, and nips my hair. I yelp and take another leap. Kenjō grabs my arm, urging me forward, but I stall and look back at the card.

"Go," I tell her. "Get out of here." I make a run for the card when a low-pitched popping sound echoes in my ears. The drakon whips its sinuous body in front of me, its mouth sneering as drool leaves its large crocodile-type fangs. I summon uruz, and my wild ox emerges from my chest, smacking the drakon in its midriff. The drakon gets flung back, but before it smacks into the wall, it disappears into the Aō.

Kenjō screams behind me, and I turn to find the drakon has reappeared and wrapped its long tail around Kenjō's body. The drakon opens its mouth, snapping closed inches in front of her face. I aim to expel uruz, but quickly decide against it as it'll hit Kenjō too. Instead, I run at them with my knife.

Kenjō's hand shifts to a jaguar's paw as she smacks the drakon across the face. The moment her claws hit, they both disappear with a loud pop into the Aō. I come to an abrupt stop and spin myself around. They're gone. No! "Kenjō?" My chest pants as panic courses through me. It's taken her into the Aō.

The silence pounds in my ears, every second that goes by means she could be eaten. I run over to the Ace of Swords. A purple glaze shimmers on the surface. The sword looks alive as if it can easily be picked up if just I reach in and grab it.

I reach for the card. An electrifying shock sends a wave of current through my body. I fall on my rear, nausea overcoming me. I force myself to stand, toppling over the podium a bit. A few words in ancient Greek are carved below the card on the mantle. They transform right before my eyes, just like my mark did when I first got here.

One worthy sacrifice to release the blade. Thence
*   returned, unless by a Fate.*

One worthy sacrifice *to* release the blade. I need to know my sacrifice before I can use it. I think.

A cacophony of noises erupts from behind me, and I spin

around. Kenjō roars as she bursts through the Aō and lands on all fours. I sprint toward her and pause when a familiar groan comes next.

Alfred plummets through the air and crashes against the stone wall. My mouth drops.

"Alfred, you came back?" He must have been following us the whole time.

Kenjō beelines toward him but I stay to meet the drakon who emerges next. Its body lengthens in size, now eclipsing the light from the entrance. The black and white strands of hair glisten from the top of its head all the way down to the tip of its tail as it sways in front of me. Sizing me up.

I glance at Kenjō's spear on the ground and make a dash to pick it up. The drakon snaps its mouth shut just as I leap away from it. I pick up the spear and clutch it in my hand, pointing it to the face of the beast. Behind it, I glimpse Alfred standing and Kenjō, still in jaguar form turning around, readying herself to attack the drakon.

"We have you surrounded, pal." I jump toward it and jab the air with the spear, missing the drakon by an inch. It whips its tail faster than I can move, and I'm thrown to my knees. With the spear still clutched in my hand, I pick myself back up. Kenjō leaps over my head, smacking the drakon across its face. The drakon headbutts Kenjō, flinging her against the wall, but she lands on her feet, only stumbling a little.

The drakon looks between us, unsure who to strike at next. I feel Alfred walking up behind me; I hold my hand out to keep him back.

This time, I summon Kenaz to the tip of the spear. The ever-burning flame; unless I put it out, it'll never go out. Kenjō moves closer to me in my peripherals, but the drakon sets its eyes on the flame. It opens its mouth and, like a snake, ready to strike, arches back.

It strikes, sending a rush of wind against my face, but just before it hits, I expel uruz. The red silhouette of a wild ox ten times my size projects out of my aura around me. Every follicle of my body burns with a powerful buzz. The drakon pushes against the ox, refusing to be flung back again. But I expected it. I just wanted it to be weaker.

It lets out a deafening roar, and just as it opens its large mouth, I throw the flaming spear right into its throat. The drakon chomps down, and for a second, I think it doesn't do anything. It stills, staring down at the floor until its body starts to shrink in size. Smoke comes out of its nose, and its eyes start to bulge. "That fire won't go out," I say. The drakon flies upward, spinning around in a frantic fury until it disappears into the Aō.

A long breath leaves my chest. I cast a look at Kenjō as she approaches me. I slant a smile at her but keep my gaze out to the center room in case it comes back. "That should kill it or keep it busy for a very long time." I look back at Alfred. "Thanks for helping Kenjō in the Aō. I don't know what I would've done if—" I stare down at her.

"Hey, Kenjō? It's gone. Why don't you shift back?"

She stares at the ground, a low growl leaving her mouth. What's that about?

"We defeated what's guarding the card," I say. "Shift back so we can talk."

She stares at me, a soft whimper leaving her lips.

"Kenjō?"

My pulse quickens. I don't like this. "Kenjō, shift back." I stare at Alfred, who's approaching her. "Why won't she shift back? Is she stuck?"

He groans loudly and places his hand on her head. I back up a little, giving them some space. The last time he touched her, he sent her to the Aō to come back having shifted. When nothing happens, he looks at me and shakes his head.

"What does that mean?" My voice rises. I go over to her and hold her head. She stares at me with those big jaguar eyes, and I swear they look sad. "Kenjō," my voice cracks. "Shift back. Please."

Her mouth opens, and she gags, blood seeping out from her tongue. My blood runs cold. No... She drops to the ground, and I drop beside her, picking her head up and putting her on my lap. Please no. Please be okay. "Kenjō, shift back. I'll carry you to Alec's Tower." Just be okay. I squeeze my eyes shut.

The whistling sound of Arcana soldiers falling from the sky comes from outside. I hold my breath. They must have sensed my magic. My eyes fall to Kenjō. "You have to get up. They'll kill you." I start to pull on her heavy jaguar form, but she doesn't budge. She doesn't even open her eyes.

"Kenjō, please...I need you to wake up. And you'll tell me all about drakons and about their magic." I hold her head to my chest, her body weight leaning on me. "And we'll have more snowball fights together." A tear runs down my cheek. "Please wake up," I croak. "So that... so that I could love you."

A moan escapes her lips, and my eyes fly open. Her moaning worsens, not the sound of someone waking, but a moaning akin to the tortured souls from the spirit forest. The air in my lungs escapes me. My hands start to shake. No. No, no, no, no. Please no. She can't be dead.

Guards burst through the entrance and surround the room. Their blank chrome faces bore into me with their soulless, empty holes for eyes.

CHAPTER SEVENTEEN

HER MOANING GROWS HOARSE. TORTURED. LEFT TO feel pain forever. And worse, she died in this form. To stay a jaguar forever. I should have realized sooner; whenever she would shift, she'd get a nosebleed. That the more she shifted, the more the Rikorō would take its course. This is all my fault.

Alfred groans loudly, and I look up. Ten Arcana soldiers stand before me. I don't care if they take me. I just don't want them to take her body. She doesn't deserve that.

I stand and step over Kenjō. One of the Arcana soldiers shoots a surge at ice to Alfred, but he disappears before it hits him. Alfred reappears behind him and claws the soldier's back. Nine of the soldiers advance toward me. Without hesitation, I summon uruz and expel the wild ox. It runs, hitting each soldier with the force of its head. Each soldier disappears, only to re-materialize moments later.

I hit them again as I walk toward them, away from Kenjō's

body. I hit them again. And again. And again. "Why aren't you fighting back?" I yell. "I'm right here!"

"That's enough," Demitri's familiar voice comes from the entrance. "They are not to kill you."

Kenjō's tortured moans ring loudly in my ears. I clench my chest with my fist. This is too much. I can't bear to hear her in pain. Knowing it's forever...

I force my gaze to Demitri standing there in his black tunic robe, tied at the waist. He's not wearing the small bishop hat this time. I part my lips and stare at Kenjō lying on the ground. I don't even know where to start to tell him about how that's her...He knows her mom, but how much does he know about their operation?

Her hoarse cries resonate through the walls.

"Grab the yeti. Don't let it get away," Demitri says. "And discard of this half-dying creature."

"Don't touch her!" *Half-dying.*

Demitri blinks at me and holds up a hand.

One of the guards shoots an ice dome around Alfred, trapping him in place. "Let him go," I yell.

"I see you defeated the drakon," he says, walking toward me. "Only a magician can do that."

Perfect timing for me to be arrested. Before I can figure out the Ace of Sword, and after what happened to Kenjō... "Let Alfred go." I flick my eyes to the soldier standing over Kenjō's body.

"That's why I let you come all this way," he says, ignoring my pleas. "We've been watching you."

Wait. What? "What do you want with *me?*"

He raises his chin. "To use your skills. I want you to come with me."

"And if I don't want to?"

He snaps his fingers, and ten soldiers stand at attention. "I'm sure I can persuade you. But I would rather you come willingly."

Right. "I don't know what you think I can do... but your Empress took my magic."

"You still lie to me after I watched you attack my soldiers repeatedly?" He says slowly.

I scan the guards standing on either side of him and steal a glance at Alfred covered in ice. That ice must be imbued with anti-Aō popping magic. "That's only a tiny bit of what I can do. Help me get my magic back, and you'll have me at your disposal. The jaguar too gets left alone, to be buried in the forest." So that she can be with her mom.

And it's not a full lie. I can try to do what he wants after I get my mother's runes back. Why go to Alec for help if I have the Empress's hierophant right here in front of me? Maybe he's the only one who can get close enough to her. "But first, let the yeti go. He's only been of help to me and.. " I swallow down the lump in my throat. "And to Kenjō."

Demitri narrows his eyes at me. "On one condition."

"What?"

"The Ace of Swords."

I flick my eyes to the card on the podium. "What about it?"

Kenjō's cries worsen, and my gut sinks below the floor. How much more of her torture can I take? How much can *she* take? She's going to be in pain forever...*Half dying.*

"Clearly, that card is why you're here," he says irritably over the jaguar's cries. "Or else you wouldn't have bothered defeating the drakon. Grab it for me."

My brows furrow. "I can't."

"Then no deal."

"I mean, I tried. It full-on zapped me."

"Hm." He chafes his chin and begins to walk to the podium. "Come with me."

I glance at Kenjō's body and reluctantly leave her to follow Demitri up the podium. A glare shines over the words: *One worthy sacrifice to release the blade. Thence returned, unless by a Fate.*

"It says, 'thence returned, unless by a fate'," Demitri declares. "And although it doesn't mention a Magician, I've always wondered if one would be powerful enough to bring it out of the temple."

I stare blankly at the encryption on the podium, then at the Ace of Swords card. Kenjō's harrowing moans cloud my thinking.

"My theory is, a Magician can carry it out of here," Demitri continues. "And that's why it comes before the order of the Empress in the Tarot. The Empress's number is three, you see?" He glares at me, and I grimace.

"Why do you want this sword so bad? Aren't you the Empress's Hierophant?"

"I don't want it for myself. I wouldn't be able to take it. But if you can take it with you, then you and I could do so much for the Empress. I've known her for many years. Once she sees your benefit, she'll place you—and I at the highest order of her court. You see... these cards were created by a Fate, but unfortunately, Her Divinity was cast out of that agreement. I think you might be the loophole. She just has to see it."

Cast out of her agreement? Kenjō's tortured moaning behind me makes my bones shake. I don't care about whatever agreement the Empress has. I agreed to do this so he'd let Alfred go and allow me to bury Kenjō where her mom is.

"Now, what about your sacrifice?"

I swallow and stare back at the sword inside the card. A purple sheen swipes the face of the card, the light from the room reflecting on the blade. I thought I was going to have to sacrifice my being with Kenjō for my chance to get to Jotunheim, to break my family's curse. Now Kenjō is gone.

My eyes flick to Kenjō's writhing, tormented body, lying almost lifeless on the ground, still in jaguar form. It's hard to imagine that this jaguar was once the clever and playful girl I met in the woods. The girl who could have turned me in instead of helping me. The girl brave enough to trust the yetis when everyone else finds them dangerous. The girl who, despite trusting her mom's cause *so* much, still didn't want to hurt anyone else.

I choke down a sob. The girl I kissed.

Her chest rises and falls as another spasm wracks her body, and I wince. I can't bear the thought of her being trapped inside that form, forever dying... Wait.

Half dying.

...She's not dead yet. She's dying.

And so is Aunt Liv. The weight of the sword pulls me down, dragging my gaze toward its perfectly sharpened tip. But maybe they don't have to be.

I turn to face Demitri. "You promise me you'll let Alfred go?"

"The yeti? Certainly. So, you'll come?"

I nod, then turn my attention to the card. *One worthy sacrifice to release the blade.*

A magnetic force tugs at my arm, and I step forward.

Kenjō's beautiful voice rings in my memory. *They say it requires a sacrifice for its magic to work.*

I know what I have to do, Kenjō.

Aunt Liv's voice rings in my memory next, *I would never want that for you. Your mother would never want that for you.* I shake her voice away. I'm sorry, Aunt Liv. I have to do this.

"What are you waiting for?" Demitri snaps. I clench my fist through its magnetic pull and reach for the card.

It's almost as if the card itself got bigger or my hand got smaller. My fingers go right between the borders. I gasp as I wrap my fingers around the sword. Taking a short step back, the sword grows to life-size proportion as I pull it completely out of the card.

"Excellent," Demitri says.

I step off the podium and walk down the steps, the hilt of the sword clutched tightly in my right hand.

I smile grimly. Kenjō, my mother, Aunt Liv, and even my father sacrificed so much for me. To keep me safe. Maybe now it's my turn.

Her tortured cries shatter my thoughts.

"Where are you going?"

"To make my sacrifice."

The Arcana soldiers stare at me as I make my way to Kenjō's half-dead body.

In this family, everything leads to death.

Tears brim my eyes, blurring my vision. My heart hammers in my throat as I kneel in front of Kenjō. I bend down and lower myself to her fierce jaguar face, despite the cries emanating from her mouth. "If this sword can truly do anything," I whisper to her ear. "It can break your curse of torment." She's not just a jaguar. She's a person. I know what'll happen. I plant a kiss on her head. "Rest in peace."

Lifting one knee, I raise the sword above her body. The ouma steel becomes almost too much for me to bear. I hear the cries of the wounded slain from its blade centuries ago. It urges my arms down to her body. I squeeze my eyes shut, and every muscle in my body tenses.

"I sacrifice myself." With one long breath, I stab her torso with the tip of the blade, letting it pierce her all the way down until it stops at the floor beneath. "May my aunt and Kenjō be free."

I hear Alfred cry out in the distance. I let myself drop to the floor as a bright light explodes from the sword and sweeps the floor. The sword rises up and crashes to the ground. I blink a few times to see Kenjō's jaguar form glowing with that same bright light. I reach out to touch her—then still in place.

An impossibly cold pain pierces through my ribs as if I had just been stabbed by a dozen icicles. I grab at my chest, but a weight pushes me to the stone floor. I open my eyes, but I'm blinded by frost. Within minutes it's gone. My knees feel weak as I stand, and my breath is cold.

My curse is enacted, and Aunt Liv is safe.

But Kenjō is dead. A shuddering breath escapes my lips as I gaze upon her jaguar form. I shroud my arms over her neck. Icy tears fall from my eyes, and I squeeze them shut. "Goodbye," I breathe. At least now, she won't suffer.

An overwhelming deafening silence comes from her body. Her tormented cries have really ended. Maybe she's still a jaguar because she died as one.

I should find solace knowing that she's finally at peace. I kiss her fur. But now she's really gone.

"Touching, now let's go. Take the sword." Demitri starts walking toward the entrance of the temple.

I force myself away from Kenjō's body to pick up the sword. Alfred can help me take her back to the cemetery. Avoiding the Arcana soldiers who stand in a line watching me as I walk to the sword that flew out of my hand and clattered on the ground, my mind goes to my mother's runes. Will I ever get them back?

"Time is running out," Demitri's voice cuts through my thoughts. "Pick up the sword."

I bend down and reach for the gold hilt of the sword. The moment I do, it zaps me like before. The sword then flies back to where the card still stands on the podium. I watch in awe as it shrinks down and reverts back to being inside the card.

I stare at Demitri. "I guess your theory's wrong. Only a Fate can take the sword with them."

Fury flashes in his eyes. He opens his mouth to speak, but a bright light comes from Kenjō's body. We both turn toward her. It glows so brightly I can no longer see any semblance of a cat.

"What's happening?" I walk over, the heat coming from the light contrasting the cold coming from my breath.

"What is this?" Demitri's voice sounds distant as the light

grows, filling the space of the room. A moment later, the light dims to only be coming from her.

The spirit of the jaguar floats over the glowing body on the floor, still covering any semblance of her. It rises in the air, then the spirit of Kenjō's Ipani form rises from the light. Her silky hair shrouds over her shoulders, barely hiding the Ipani stripes on her neck and arms. Her subtly pointed ears peak out from her hair. Her eyes are closed. My breath catches.

Then, in an instant, the jaguar bursts into hundreds of specs of light, falling onto the stone floor. I hold my breath as Kenjō's spirit falls slowly back into her body.

Kenjō's body—her beautiful Ipani body, lies on the stone floor. I gasp. Although she isn't moving, I have a sliver of hope. I run over to her and drape my arms over her chest, icy tears falling freely on my face.

She moves, and my chest starts to pound.

"You're alive?" I croak.

She stirs in my arms and blinks a few times. "H-Harold?" Her beautiful brown eyes glare back at me. I brush her cheek with the back of my hand. I can't believe it. "H-how?"

She sniffles and sits up. "I-I can't feel it anymore. The Rikorō."

"I released you," I whisper. "The beast and the Rikorō don't control you anymore. You are free."

Her breath hitches, and she darts a glance at the Ace of Swords. "You killed the jaguar. But... your mother's runes. Your family's curse."

I shake my head. "I took care of it." I reach to bring her face back to mine and lean in for a kiss. Her warm lips press against mine, my icy breath chilling her slightly.

Demitri's steel boots echo on the stone floor. "Kenjō, you were the jaguar?" His eyes fall on me. She winces.

Holding her arms tight, I help her onto her feet. Alfred groans loudly in the background, and I flick my eyes to him, still being trapped by ice.

"You said you'd let him go."

He narrows his eyes. "No sword, no deal." He snaps his fingers and turns to leave. "Take him and the yeti both."

My eyes widen. "Wait. Where are you taking me?"

Demitri smirks over his shoulder. "Your ship leaves in an hour."

"What ship?"

A soldier appears from behind me. I stare at Kenjō, who's still getting used to her balance.

Demitri turns to another soldier. "Take Kenjō home."

The soldier grabs me and rips my grasp away from Kenjō's hand. She cries out my name, but in a gust of white smoke, I'm taken away.

CHAPTER EIGHTEEN

It takes me minutes to get my bearings. Between the thick smoke from the Arcana soldiers and the disorientation from being—teleported? My head is fuzzy. What I do know is that I'm in a dark room and on my hands and knees.

The last thing I saw was Kenjō reaching for me, fear stricken as she called out my name.

Coughing comes from somewhere beside me.

"Hello?" I try to stand, but the ground still seems to be moving. I topple backward and hit my head on what feels like metal. Ouch. I pull myself up and get thrown forward, hitting myself on metal bars. Gripping my fingers between the metal, I reach above my head, grabbing onto more metal bars. I'm inside a large cage.

And the floor is definitely moving; I thought it was nausea. It's coming back to me now. Demitri said my ship leaves in an hour. I grab onto my belt and gasp. It's gone. They took Kenjō's potion bottles. I had forgotten about them. A door creaks a few paces away, allowing a sliver of light to seep through. Heavy boots step onto the wood floor, followed by the lighting of a match and a gas lamp illuminating the area. To my right are two cages with Ipani people in them, one guy and one girl. The guy coughs a few times but closes his eyes.

Two men enter through the doorway and make their way to the first cage with the girl in it. The first man has a big gut and a pointy nose. The second is tall and lanky and wears a leather version of a beanie on his head. They sort of remind me of the Penguin and the Riddler.

The lanky Riddler pulls out a heavy wool sheet from the back of some crates and drapes it over the girl's cage. They do the same with the male Ipani's cage.

The two men exchange a few words in a language I can't understand as they help each other carry each crate out of the room. They're both human, so I'm guessing it must be Imboe unless they both speak Ipani. But if they're speaking Imboe, why can't I understand them? I swallow a gasp. The translation potion must have left my system. I knew it was going to happen but talk about terrible timing.

Something catches my attention on my left wrist, and I lower my sleeve. What the heck? A small "O" appears as a birthmark. We can have two marks? I check my right wrist. The Magician's mark is still there.

Interesting. This "O" as being The Fool. I smile to myself. Makes sense. If this world marks everyone based on who they are, there's no shadow of the doubt that I'm the fool. But why now and not sooner?

At least now I know my aunt will be okay. And Kenjō is alive.

The door opens wider, and in steps a woman wearing a long red leather coat and a brown pirate hat on her head, decorated with a black feather. She has long, black curly hair tied behind her, and earrings decorate her human ears from top to bottom. I grip the metal bars as she strides my way.

She tells me something in what I can assume is Imboe. The only two things I pick up are Demitri and Kenjō. I arch a brow at the mention of Kenjō's name, and her lips curl into a smile. How does she know Kenjō? Wait, Kenjō mentioned her Ama was a human, and a merchant, which makes sense that she's a pirate who disguises her trade. Wasn't she docking soon? And Demitri knows her too. My eyes widen. Odin's balls, this is Kenjō's mother, Bronte.

"Where are you taking me?" I ask.

Bronte screws up her face and shakes her head. She snaps her fingers, and Penguin and lanky Riddler come up behind her. Lanky Riddler pulls out a pair of keys and starts opening the lock. I bring my arm back and call upon uruz. The pirates stop and stare at me.

Nothing happens. I chalk it off to being tired, and this time when trying again, I muster all my energy and scream, "Uruz."

The only thing that happens is frost forming at my fingertips and icy cold breath in my mouth. The captain and her two sidekicks laugh. The blood drains from my face. When I willfully enacted my curse as my sacrifice, it must have wiped me out of my connection to the runes too.

"No..." I step back as the lanky Riddler reaches in and grabs me. I kick him hard in the chest, to be met with a blow to my eye. He pulls out a syringe, and I try to fight him, but they both close in on me inside the cage. With both of them fighting me, they eventually stab me in the neck. I fall back. My eyes grow heavy as I watch them leave the room. Bronte is the last one to leave, and she snuffs the oil lamp on her way out, leaving me in the dark. My limbs are numb, I can't move, but I can still think.

No matter where I'm going, I'll get myself out of this. I will get my mother's runes back, and I will bond with them again. I don't know how, and I don't know when. But I will make it to Jotunheim to lift my family's curse. Not only to save my own life but for anyone else who comes after me.

Find out what happens to Harold in *The Cursed Tarot*, the first installment of the *Chronicles of Tarotland* series.

THANK YOU

Thank you so much for reading *The Fool's Journey!* I hope you enjoyed Harold's adventure in the Isle of Swords as much as I loved writing it. Find out what becomes of Harold in my Alice in Wonderland retelling, *The Cursed Tarot.*

If you would like to receive updates on all my new releases, please join my mailing list at http://killianwolf.com/. You will also get access to my books at a discounted launch price when they first come out, along with an exclusive sneak peek or short story just for you.

GET IN TOUCH!

Come say hi in my Facebook Reader group. In there, every day is Halloween!

facebook.com/groups/killianwolf

Please feel free to get in touch with me.

Website: http://killianwolf.com/

facebook.com/killianwolfauthor

twitter.com/killian_wolf22

instagram.com/killian_wolf_author

pinterest.com/killianwolf22

goodreads.com/killianwolf

amazon.com/Killian-Wolf/e/B07WHFB8FW

bookbub.com/authors/killian-wolf

tiktok.com/@killian_wolf_author

patreon.com/killianwolfauthor

ACKNOWLEDGMENTS

As far as reader magnets go, this one's the longest I've ever written. Harold's story began as a ten-thousand-word idea and quickly became a sixty-thousand-word novel during NaNoWriMo. I wrote it alongside The Cursed Tarot, and it was often in an open document for random spurts of dialogue between Harold and Kenjō. And yet, this book could not be what it is without the help of some wicked awesome people.

To Ash the Silent, thank you for being my rune teacher all those years ago. To this day, I live by them.

To my Guildmates at our Writer's Guild- Claerie, Emily, Christina, and Shermon; thank you for critiquing the hell out of this story and making me re-write chapters until the pacing was right. This book wouldn't be what it is without you.

A special thanks to Christian Thalmann. Your creation of the Ipani language has been a huge contribution to the cultures of Ipa and a lot of what makes the characters special. I look forward to continuing working with you.

To my husband for your remarkable patience and for being a beta reader. You caught so many mistakes my tired eyes couldn't. Thank you, and I love you.

Thanks to Odin for inspiring me to write Harold's story as he learns the wisdom of the runes while wandering the world of Ipa and for the inspiration to write his spin-off series that's to come.

Lastly, a thank you to my readers, especially the ones making it all the way here. I hope you enjoyed reading these characters as much as I loved writing them.

ABOUT THE AUTHOR

Killian Wolf is a Miami, Florida, native who enjoys pirates, rum, and skulls as much as she loves writing about dark magick and sorcerers. She holds a Bachelor of Arts degree in Cultural Anthropology and Sociology and a Master of Science in Environmental Archaeology and Palaeoeconomy.

Killian writes books about obtaining magickal powers and stepping into other dimensions. She lives in Florida with her husband, a tornado of a cat, and the most timid snake you'd ever meet. When she isn't writing, you might find her at an archaeological dig, rock climbing, or sipping on dark spiced rum while working on a painting.

GLOSSARY

IPANI VOCABULARY

Āngaraeke: *Yeti*

Buchiveru: *stabilizer, plant*

Drakon: *Ancient Greek dragon with a serpentine body. Can both swim and fly, and pop in and out of the Aō dimension.*

È: *Sound often used by natives of Piupeki, used to represent a sound made in speech in a variety of situations, often used to ask for something to be repeated or explained or to elicit agreement.*

Garisi: *Drinkable potion, as opposed to explosive potion*

Hn: *A sound made by an Ipani when thinking out loud.*

Imboe: [im.boe] *Ancient Greek-Ipani creole spoken in Ipa.*

Indakepoa : [ˌin.da.ke.ˈpoa] *Translation potion, liquorice*

Ipani: [i.ˈpa.ni] *Of the World; the language of the World. Ipani (singular and plural)*

Ko: *Negative, soft no*

Koj: *No, Don't*

Muse: [ˈmu.se] *Spider*

Ouma: [ˈow.ma] *Magic; magical*

Oumala: [ow.ˈma.la] *Mage, practitioner of magic, magic user*

Oete: [ˈoe.t̥ e] *"Move"*

Rikorō: [ˈdik.oro] *Soul thief, plant*

Solerie: [so.le.ˈrie] *Soleri'g, solerigo (i) peppermint (lit.: ice-leaf), give you transparency, spectre, can be used for people and objects*

Temū: [te.ˈmuː] *"Walk"*

PLACES

Aō: [a.ˈo] *World spirit*

Ahan Alēla: *Ghost forest, haunted forest*

Ipa: [ˈee.pa] *The global ocean, the World*

Naó: *Greek Temple*

Pea Memoé: *"Eternal Mountains"*

Peki Guí: *"Ear rock" Village to the west of the island*

Piupeki: *"Steelrock" Island farthest to the North. Currently called Swords, Piupeki by the rebels.*

Rutavenye: *"Cloudwall" The Floating island, location of The Tower*

PHRASE

Koj urte: *Don't move*
Twae po: *Who are you?*